LAZLO'S STRIKE

LAZLO'S STRIKE

T. V. Olsen

GUNSMOKE

First published in the UK by Hale

This hardback edition 2010
by BBC Audiobooks Ltd
by arrangement with
Golden West Literary Agency

ISBN 978 1 408 46242 3

British Library Cataloguing in Publication Data available.

To Dorothy Guilday

Printed and bound in Great Britain by
CPI Antony Rowe, Chippenham and Eastbourne

CHAPTER 1

The one-room stone jail was pierced by a single small high window. As the sun got higher, a narrow shaft of light crawled down the inside wall and touched the cheek of the sleeper sprawled on a straw pallet on the bare dirt floor.

Lazlo Kusik groaned. His bearded face twitched. He came by miserable and grudging degrees out of a deep well of sleep, shrugging away the frayed horse blanket under which he'd huddled through most of a freezing night he · could hardly remember. Then he edged to a sitting position, holding his head and shuddering with agony.

Now he did begin to remember, and it made him groan again.

Over by the wall opposite him, Hutch Prouter was stirring on his own moldy pallet. He cocked open one eye and turned his shaggy head enough to give Lazlo a raffish wink.

"How do there, little pard?" said Hutch. "Man, you do look like hell."

Lazlo planted a hand against the scarred wall and maneuvered gradually to his feet. When he'd made it, he teetered unsteadily. He knew exactly how Sisera would have felt if, by some unwelcome magic, he could have survived with that spike driven through his skull.

Nice thought. It drew a third tortured groan out of him.

Hutch Prouter yawned and patted his great tub of a belly. He sat upright on his heap of straw, combed a hamlike hand through his curly thatch of blond hair, and said agreeably, "God's own truth, ain't it? Know just how you feel. 'Bout now you be afraid you gonna die. One hour from now you will be afraid you ain't gonna."

Lazlo eyed him with a sick resentment. "You had as much to drink as me," he managed to croak. "That is, I think you had as much."

"Ain't that God's truth," Hutch said cheerfully. "I had more'n that, little pard, a whole heap more. But my plumbing is fixed for it, you see. It is used to taking on mebbe a half gallon o' tanglefoot ever' night. The godawful lizard pee they serve up in this camp do take some getting used to, what I mean."

Then too, maybe Hutch was just plain built for taking on a load of that kind and quantity. As he stood up now, scraping wisps of straw out of his hair, Hutch's head was an inch short of brushing a ceiling beam. It was a broad jug of a head that went perfectly with his huge, imposing frame. That, along with his sway-bellied front and the layers of tallowy fat over his massive musculature, reminded you of an overgrazed bull in a pasture. Even the bunch of crinkling curls over his forehead resembled a bull's poll. Hutch was about thirty.

Still holding both hands to his head, Lazlo Kusik shuffled shakily up and down the ten-by-fifteen-foot floor of the jailhouse and tried to collect his thoughts. Damn Hutch Prouter anyway.

How much did I say to him last night? Lazlo wondered dismally. How much did I tell him?

The battering hurt of his head made it impossible to sort out many details just yet. Memories of last night all flowed together in a fragmented mishmash.

Later. Maybe it would all come clear for him later.

How long had they been in this place? Lazlo couldn't even remember being hauled off to jail or the events that had led up to it. He patted his pockets. Amazingly, all their usual contents were in place. At least he hadn't been "rolled." His knife sheath was empty and his rifle was missing. But that was to be expected.

Pacing up and down, fighting not to retch, he tried to get up a painful interest in the gloomy interior of their cell. He had never seen the inside of Bozetown's little stone-walled jail before, and he decided it was about as interesting as slow death.

It contained a single slop bucket and a few straw pallets for overnight inmates, and that was all. The stones were so poorly mortared together that probably a few husky men could set their shoulders and push out a wall, and one man could tunnel out under the same wall in a few hours. However, hardly anyone ever bothered to.

Who needed a secure jail for a flare-up, die-fast camp like Bozetown?

The gold-strike camp was barely a year old and might not last another year. The usual way of dealing with a felony such as stealing a mule or salting and selling a bad claim—murder and actual claim-jumping ranked somewhat behind those injustices—was at the big hanging tree on the edge of town. Minor transgressions of various kinds earned you a night in the pokey. The lines were pretty clear-cut; there was no reason to bother with the niceties of a judge or jury.

A key rattled in the padlock that secured the oak-slab door. It swung open. A stocky man with a traplike jaw stood in the sudden blaze of sunlight.

The two prisoners blinked at him owlishly.

"Abe Friendly," Hutch greeted him, "you look just awful this morning. Christ, do you ever!"

Marshal Friendly was not amused. He swung out of the doorway and jerked his head sideways. "Out," he said.

They picked up their hats and tramped out past him, the sun hurting their eyes.

"What the Christ time is it?" asked Hutch.

"Hard onto the hour of noon. You two was dead to the world when the sun come up, so I let you sleep. Here—"

Marshal Friendly was toting Lazlo's rifle under his arm. He gave it to him, and pulled Lazlo's Bowie knife from his belt and handed that over. Then he returned Hutch's pocket knife and his Whitneyville Walker Colt, a vintage weapon with most of the bluing worn off its long barrel.

Lazlo inspected the mechanism of his rifle, feeling a nudge of shame even in his physical misery. He remembered practically nothing of last night but was reasonably sure that some of his behavior hadn't been all wool and a yard wide.

"Marshal," he said tentatively, "I hope I did not—"

"Not much, you didn't. You had yourself quite a snootful. First time I ever seen you kick up a ruckus, Kusik."

Lazlo grunted, feeling a little more sickish.

"You shot off seven of them ornamental wood knobs on the sign Dick Slade has over his saloon. Eight shots, and you missed one." Marshal Friendly's voice held neither censure nor interest. "Fair shooting for a man who couldn't walk a straight line anymore."

"Oh, Laz is a seven-day wonder when he is good and likkered. Say there, Abe Friendly"—Hutch gave a broad wink as he rammed the pistol into the waistband of his greasy leather pants—"what's chances for the law giving us a good breakfast. Customary thing, ain't it?"

The marshal gave him a steely-eyed look. Abe Friendly was only a provisional official, hired by Bozetown's vigilante committee to handle troublemakers in the camp proper. He had a long and varied background as a peace officer; now he was gray and getting a hint of paunch, but you never doubted he could still handle himself in the clutch.

"It's waiting for you over there." He pointed his thumb at a nearby horsetrough. "Fill up."

He turned on his heel and walked away.

"Now don't that beat all kinds of generosity four ways to hell!" Hutch let out a throaty roar of laughter, then smacked a massive palm between Lazlo's shoulders, staggering him. "Well, we can rinse our heads out anyways, hey, little pard? Then, I will allow you to buy me breakfast. What say?"

On wobbly legs Lazlo followed his hulking companion over to the horsetrough. They knelt down beside it and ducked their heads. The water was clear and icy-cold, being piped from a mountain stream above the camp and also having an outlet pipe from the trough. That made it all right to drink the water too.

At least Lazlo hoped so, for he had a burning thirst. He drank long and deep.

When he straightened up, he mopped his face dry with a

pocket bandanna and felt a little better. At least the fuzz was out of his brain as well as his mouth. He slid Hutch Prouter a wary glance as the latter heaved to his feet, spluttering like a walrus.

Again Lazlo thought worriedly: What did I tell him? How much?

He suspected that if he *had* spilled any of the beans, he might have good reason to worry. He didn't know Hutch very well and couldn't call him a friend. Last night they had joined forces for a monumental drunken tear—the first of its kind in a short and casual acquaintance.

What Lazlo did know, or had heard on pretty good authority, was that Hutch had a kind of unruly reputation. Nothing quite on the outright shady side, but more than a little rascally.

Hutch dressed with slovenly indifference. He wore dirty rawhide trousers and an equally dirty cowhide vest over dirty red flannel underwear—no shirt. He topped off the ensemble with a filthy battered hat. All of it went with the expression on his face, which was thick and stupid.

Except for the eyes. They were chill as ice, and for all his constant banter, they never lost that sly and searching look. You had the feeling that nothing much got by Hutch Prouter. Nothing, that is, which could be turned to Hutch's advantage.

"How 'bout that breakfast now?" Hutch patted his great kettle gut. "Man, I could put away a whole steer off the hoof by my own self. But I'll split 'im down the middle with you iffen you can dig up the wherewithal."

Lazlo's stomach gave a queasy lurch. He grimaced and shook his head.

"I know how you feel, little pard, and that's God's truth. But a mite o' grub will serve to settle your innards, take it from ole Hutch."

"I think I must get back to my claim," Lazlo protested. "I have work to do. Also, I came to town to buy a wagon and a team . . ."

"And not get full o' redeye, hey?" Hutch chuckled. "Hell, it done you good. Man is got to get loosed up oncet in a while.

'Nother hour or so 'fore you get back to your digs ain't gonna
hurt none. That claim ain't gonna up and fly away on you
meantime . . ."

As he spoke, Hutch took Lazlo's arm and effortlessly pro-
pelled him down Bozetown's single dirt street.

"Got a mite o' coin left in my own poke," Hutch went on,
"and I will spend it to settle your bad belly iffen you will do as
much for my empty one. What say?"

There wasn't much Lazlo could say against the clamp of
Hutch's powerful hand on his arm. Worry that he might arouse
Hutch's curiosity by protesting too much overrode his uneasy
wish to have no more to do with the man. Also, he was as sick
as a dog. So he let himself be dragged along.

The morning was still brisk and even a touch chilly, although the sun was high above the ramshackle sprawl of Bozetown. A typical gold-strike camp, it had been laid out for expe-
diency, not permanence. The whole town was built in gulches
and on slopes, so that many of the shacks and buildings that
composed it were set above or below others. A man couldn't
stand on his own doorstep and take a healthy piss without putting out the fire in his neighbor's chimney, or so went the saying. Since the female population of Bozetown was almost nil,
that was more than mere speculation; it was a downright possibility.

The muddy squalor of the camp was in contrast to the rise
of timbered foothills above and around it and the soaring gran-
deur of the Elk Mountains against a clean blue sky beyond.
The majestic sweep of nature dwarfed and swallowed man's little effacements.

Lazlo Kusik never contemplated the virgin vastness of this
mountain country without feeling properly awed and humbled.
There were mountains in Hungary, too, but they were faint in
his memory. His parents had departed the old country when he
was five or six . . . and for nearly twenty years afterward he
had known only the swarming ghettoes of New York's Lower
East Side. Then there was five years of following the wheat
harvests on the flat plains of the Middle West.

Yes . . . this western land was still awesome country to a

Hungarian immigrant. Lazlo Kusik had lived in its wilds for several years now, had come to know it a little, and had learned how to cope with its rough and savage ways. But it was still bigger than any man could hope to know, even in a lifetime.

Hutch headed straight for the Hoodoo Bar, tramping in ahead of Lazlo at his rolling swagger, elbowing apart the batwing doors.

"Hey there, Aussie!" Hutch's booming voice caromed around the stale confinement of the Hoodoo's log walls. "How's chances for a snort o' the dog's hair this early? What say?"

Aussie Stubbs was a sallow runt of a Sydney Duck who, like many of his countrymen, had come to work in the American gold fields. He'd decided almost at once that at gold-camp prices, there were easier ways to make a living. Aussie had set up a saloon and charged his own prices.

"Coming right up, gents." Aussie promptly left his task of sweeping the packed-dirt floor and stepped behind his plank bar. "Couple of 'Shawn O'Farrells,' will it be?"

"That'll do capital. Belly up, little pard."

The suggestion stirred Lazlo's churning stomach juices almost to eruption. "I do not think that would be a good idea . . ."

Hutch peered at him closely. "Why hell's bells, Laz. You are green to the gills, boy, and no mistake. Aussie, you got a can o' tomatoes handy? And maybe a raw egg?"

"Right on 'and, guv'nor. But the egg'll cost yer. They're fifty cents apiece, you know."

"I know, you little gouging Limey pipsqueak," Hutch said affably. He slapped some coins on the bar. "There's the color o' my goods. Let's see yourn."

Lazlo, his eyes glazed with internal anguish, watched without interest as Hutch razored open the can with his pocket knife, fished out the tomatoes, and popped them one by one into his mouth, then broke the egg into the juice, and with a spoon provided by Aussie whipped them to a sickly seeming mixture.

"There now, little pard. You drink up. This will get you settled for somp'n better. God's own truth!"

Lazlo gazed at the proffered can in Hutch's paw. He shuddered, and decided quite abruptly that even if it made him sicker, the result might be therapeutic. He grabbed the can and drained its contents.

To his amazement, his internal churnings subsided a little. But this made him even more aware of his pounding headache.

As if having read his mind, Hutch said, "Aw right now, you take that 'Shawn O'Farrell.' Down the hatch with 'er."

Aussie had set out two shotglasses, a bottle of whiskey, and two glasses of beer. He poured whiskey into each shotglass, cocking a sympathetic eye at Lazlo. "'Aven't 'ad your scuppers awash too often, 'ave yer, chum?"

Taking it to be a query as to his drinking habits, Lazlo shook his head.

"Well then, you take this old rumpot's word and do like your mate says. Close your eyes and swill 'er straight down. In no time yer'll be 'earing chimes sweeter'n the bow bells."

"Painter sweat first"—Hutch tossed down his whiskey in a gulp—"then your lizard pee. See?" He drank the beer straight off too.

Lazlo thought it might be best not to think about it too long. He laid his rifle on the bar, wiped a shaking hand over his mouth, and picked up the shotglass. He nearly gagged on the raw whiskey, but got it down and then took the beer, drinking it down carefully but steadily.

Aussie folded his thin arms and leaned them on the bar, grinning a little. "You done up the town for fair last night, you two."

Hutch poured himself another slug of whiskey. "Yeah, I 'member some of it. Shot up a few things, didn't we?"

"Right you are, guv'nor. This chum of yours is some 'andsome marksman. 'E ought to enter the competition."

"He can handle a long gun mighty peart," Hutch agreed, pouring a third whiskey. "What competition's that?"

"Take it you chaps 'aven't 'eard. There's a show come to

town that set up business yesterday, over on 'Umbug Flat. Colonel Laban Ruddy's Medicine Circus, it calls itself."

"What the hell is a medicine circus?"

"As it 'appens, yours truly took in yesterday's performance. What it amounts to is a patent-medicine spiel with a few sideshows to it. Today, among other things, there's to be a wrestling match and a rifle shoot."

"Hey, you hear that, little pard?" Hutch delivered a mighty slap to Lazlo's back. "Shooting and wrassling! Don't it sound to you like them's right up our alleys?"

This time Lazlo didn't stagger, even though the slap had more force than its predecessor. He stood straight at the bar and turned another look at Hutch.

The "Shawn O'Farrell" had gone down as smooth as honey, and a small miracle had taken place. Lazlo felt like his usual self again. Which was to say, stern and straight-headed and not about to take an ounce of guff off anyone. In fact, his ordinary sobriety ended just short of surliness. He was known by the few who knew him at all as a gruff and short-spoken man.

His legs were braced solidly apart; his stocky and muscular body barely stirred to Hutch's thick-handed blow. His stare held a black warning light that made Hutch drop his hand.

"Well say," Hutch said with a kind of lame grin, "you're looking a heap better already, Laz."

Lazlo nodded, holding his stance and stare. "That is what you call the dog's hair, eh?"

"Yeah, well, hair o' the dog, really. Sets a body's humors right up, don't it?"

Lazlo nodded once more, gravely. He lifted his rifle off the bar. "Now I will go home to my claim."

"Hold on there, little pard—" Hutch swung his massive front away from the bar, facing Lazlo. "Let's chaw this business over a mite . . ."

"Breakfast?" Lazlo flicked the faintest of smiles. "I don't need any. You go have yours. All thanks to you for the dog's hair . . . and the other."

"No, dammit! I mean them shooting and wrassling matches

Aussie heard tell about. Why shoot, boy, them could be tailor-made for you 'n' me! I'll do the fighting and you do the firing. We will lay bets on ourselves with the crowd and . . . hell, man, we can really clean up!"

Lazlo shrugged. "What is the need?"

Hutch's eyes narrowed; he gave a hitch to his paunch-sagged trousers. "You told me last night you was so busted you didn't know if you could last out in these parts for 'nother month. Said you hadn't sluiced up hardly no color a-tall of late. Told me so five, six times as I recall. You telling me now that you ain't in need?"

So that is what I told him! Lazlo thought with a flood of relief. *But maybe I went too far with it . . .*

Maybe. Just maybe he had. A man's suspicions could be touched as readily by a vehement denial as by an outright assertion. Lazlo wondered if he had done as much with Hutch Prouter.

Damn his own whiskey-loosened tongue! He was relieved that Hutch was ignorant of the reality, but now he must be careful about what he said.

"You are very sure you and me can win."

"Betcher ass I am!" Hutch raised a hand to clap it down on Lazlo's shoulder, but then thought better of it and dropped the hand. "Why hell, betwixt us we can whup the socks offen any sucker in this damn camp! I seen how you can shoot, and by grab I know what I can do in a wrassling fall. Now then—whaddaye think?"

"I think I will have another whiskey."

Grinning, Aussie poured him another drink.

Lazlo fingered the shotglass, turning it gently in his work-toughened hand. He studied his own reflection in the stained mirror above Aussie's shoulder. Hutch beside him made Lazlo look like a midget, but he wasn't really all that undersize.

Lazlo was a little under average height, square-faced, and wide in the chest and shoulders. His hair was dark brown and curly, clipped close to his head, and his short beard followed the contour of a determined jaw. His swarthy skin was weathered to the darkness of mahogany. His nose was stubby from being twice broken in brawls that had been forced on him because he carried himself too taut and straight to suit the tastes of some belligerent types he'd run into. His eyebrows almost met above his nose, forming a thick straight bar.

His clothes were those of any working miner: a gray flannel shirt, heavy pants tucked into sturdy boots, a battered hat that was weathered to an indeterminate color. If his worn garments differed in any way from those of most of his fellow prospectors, it was that his own were fairly clean, also neatly patched and mended—by Lazlo's own hand.

"One thing you did not think of," he said quietly.

"What's 'at?"

"Money. We cannot get up enough between us to make any bets we place worth the while."

"No need to, guv," said Aussie, still grinning as he glanced from one of them to the other. "I got a good feeling about you two gents . . . and old Aussie 'as never been one as flinches from a strong 'unch. Think I'll ride this 'ere one out. You chaps do the honors in the ring . . . and I'll circulate through the crowd and lay bets for all of us. We'll split the winnings three ways. What say?"

"I say you could stand to lose your shirt," Lazlo said dryly.

"Naw he don't!" roared Hutch. "Come on, Laz. *You* don't stand to lose a damn thing, leastways. And you sure's hell could use the money. What about it?"

Lazlo gazed impassively into his glass. He had no wish to engage in a spate of foolish theatrics for the little extra money it might bring him. He was impatient to get back to his gold claim . . . and something else that was a whole lot bigger.

But again, suppose his refusal were to kindle Hutch's suspicions? It stood to reason that a man who needed money as badly as he did—or as he'd told Hutch he did—couldn't afford to turn down an opportunity as certain as this one. Not when he could handle a rifle as well as Lazlo Kusik could.

Unable to think of any likely excuse, he shrugged and took his second whiskey in a swallow. Then he said curtly, "Yes. Done."

CHAPTER 2

Yesterday Lazlo had come to Bozetown to buy what he needed to implement his plan. This included a wagon and team, some sawed lumber, carpentry tools, and more grub supplies. Yet he'd been sidetracked all too soon.

Ordinarily Lazlo wasn't much of a drinker. But the weeks of work and worry had taken their toll of him. With his tense nerves, he could use a slug of whiskey. Quite a few, in fact: he was in a mood to pull out all stops. So the rest of the day, and most of the night as well, had been lost in a swirl of liquor fumes and drunken doings. He had bought a lot of drinks for saloon hangers-on at every whiskey dive in Bozetown.

Somewhere along the way he had picked up Hutch Prouter. It couldn't have seemed too ominous a development at the time, for Hutch was a carousing companion second to none. He'd known how to turn a modestly good time into a tremendous time; he had suggested all kinds of crazy things that he and Lazlo could do to hooraw the camp.

All Lazlo could do now was to damn his own stupidity for tying one on last night . . .

The humpy stretch of Humbug Flat, just east of town, hardly deserved the name of a flat. But it was the nearest patch of land around Bozetown that resembled one. Quite a lot of the camp people and a number of miners were gathered there by the time Lazlo, Hutch, and Aussie arrived on the scene.

"Blinkin' show didn't pull all this much of a crowd yesterday," Aussie told his companions. "Word 'as got around by now. The colonel's a good 'un, all right. Wait'll yer see 'im in action. Show ought to be starting about now."

The crowd was fairly large, quite boisterous, and all male. A lot of the boys were fortifying themselves from jugs and bottles which they passed around freely and openly. They were out for a good time and were likely to get fractious if the day's offerings failed to provide one.

The traveling show's facilities of shelter and transportation consisted of three large wagons, walled and roofed and painted a bright red. On their sides the legend "Colonel Ruddy's Medicine Circus" was painted in garish yellow curlicues.

"What the hell does that say?" asked Hutch.

He was surprised when Lazlo easily read the words aloud for him.

A self-taught reader himself, Lazlo had found lots of time since his illiterate boyhood to school himself in printed English. What else did a man do with his days during the long months of being holed up in lonely winter quarters of one kind or another? It was either spend your time reading or else go crazy.

The three wagons were pulled up in a line facing the open stretch of ground where the crowd was milling. The tall back of one wagon was hinged at the bottom; disengaged at the top, it had been swung down to a horizontal position and propped up with blocks to form a little stage platform. Behind the platform, thick curtains of shabby purple velour hid the wagon's interior.

Now the curtains parted. A man stepped out, raising his arms for silence.

When he got a partial compliance, he boomed out: "Welcome, gentlemen! Welcome to our medicine circus. I am Colonel Laban Ruddy."

The colonel was short and paunchy; his gestures were as florid as his face, which was networked with the conspicuous veins of a heavy drinker. All the same, when done up in the latest spit and style of flamboyant fashion, with his fine coat of blue broadcloth opened to a flowered waistcoat, he had a certain dignity of mien. He wore his white hair longish under a pearl-gray Stetson. His white goatee chopped up and down to the sonorous roll of his words.

With many dramatic gestures, Colonel Ruddy told of how a

few years ago he had come into possession of the closely guarded secrets of the Medewiwin, the medicine society of the great Ojibway nation of the north. These had been revealed to him by a famous shaman of the tribe, "O-jik-wa-ko-bis," as a token of gratitude after Colonel Ruddy had saved the revered medicine man's life.

". . . and the therapeutic virtues of those secrets can be yours as well, my friends! From 'O-jik-wa-ko-bis' himself I learned the intricate processes of wedding rare herbs of the northern tundras into a potion of miraculous properties. Administered in regular doses, it is a decoction guaranteed to alleviate every malaise to which the flesh of humanity is heir. Momentarily"—the colonel swept up one hand in a histrionic flourish—"you shall witness with your own eyes the dramatic truth of that statement . . ."

"Hey, where's the princess?" someone yelled.

Cheers and whistles from the crowd.

Colonel Ruddy paused, smiling, his hand still upraised. "You anticipate me, sir. But first—I was about to say—I present for your entertainment and delectation a most remarkable demonstration of the terpsichorean art, brought from the mysterious reaches of the Circassian East—land of the savage and the sensuous! From the wild steppes of the Russian Caucasus, I give you the exotic charms of . . . the Princess Shahazar!"

The curtain behind him parted. The colonel bowed and stepped aside as a girl came out on the platform.

She was an eyeful, all right. She had corn-yellow hair piled high on her small head, and her eyes were bright blue above a wisp of veil designed to titillate rather than to conceal. The "Circassian" reference must have been thrown in to explain her light eyes and hair and—so Lazlo guessed—circumvent any erudite nitpicker in the audience who might have the temerity to doubt her Eastern origin.

Not that anyone in this crowd was likely to be interested in questioning a damn thing.

The girl began to do a slow, swaying, sinuous dance that lived up pretty well to the colonel's introductory spiel. Well enough, that is, in a mechanical sort of way. She wore a deep scoop-necked bodice that left her midriff bare and a pair of thin baggy trousers made of some shiny stuff that left her lower legs and feet bare. Metal bangles on her wrists and ankles tinkled to her light, graceful movements.

Undeniably the Princess Shahazar was a very pretty girl, and very well built for being so slim. Rather too slim, Lazlo thought: "thin" might be a better word. He did not think she looked altogether healthy. The fall afternoon had warmed up some by now, yet the princess's pale skin was goosefleshed with cold. A couple of times she tried to stifle coughs and didn't quite succeed. After her first voluptuous impact wore off, she seemed to be just a waif of a girl—and she couldn't be over sixteen.

If any other onlooker shared his thoughts, Lazlo saw no sign of it. The crowd stood gaping and avid. When the princess had finished her dance, the storm of applause brought her back for a couple of lengthy encores before they'd permit her to retire.

Now in a good humor, the audience warmed up to Colonel Ruddy's medicine spiel. He repeated with a few elaborations more or less what he'd said before. This time he capped his introductory remarks with the dramatic announcement that the shaman "O-jik-wa-ko-bis," as a favor to his white friend and blood brother, had sent with him on this medicine tour no other than his own son, "Wa-nit-ka-we-bo," to uphold Colonel Ruddy's true words.

At this, an Indian youth clad in white buckskins stepped from behind the curtains and stood gravely by, arms folded. The sight of him sent a ripple of chuckles through the crowd.

"Wa-nit-ka-we-bo" was about the oddest-looking specimen of the Indian race that Lazlo had ever seen. He had a big head with a flat, broad moon face that was set on top of a wiry, spindly body. Yet when he opened his mouth and spoke, he was almost magically transformed. Suddenly he was a Presence, eloquent and commanding. Gravely, in a deeply modulated voice and in flawless English, he declared that the words of the friend of his father were true words.

And so on.

Lazlo couldn't fault the Indian's performance, but one or

two things about him didn't ring quite true. He was too young to show the signs of heavy drinking as much as Ruddy did, but there they were all the same: a hint of bloat in the broad features, a touch of rheuminess in the eye. And what about the way he talked? Lazlo had to cudgel his memory to recall where in the devil he'd come across the likes of it before. Suddenly he knew. Yes. "Wa-nit-ka-we-bo's" style of speech was straight out of James Fenimore Cooper's *Leatherstocking Tales*.

It didn't matter to the crowd. Maybe half of them were taken in, while the other half was having a hell of a good time and wasn't about to spoil the fun.

Colonel Ruddy took center stage once more, this time with a harder-line spiel for his "Celebrated Ojibway Elixir and Vermifuge," at a good gold-camp price: four dollars a bottle. A wizened gaffer of a prospector named Briggs, who'd often complained of his pestiferous gout, bought the first bottle. He took a big swig of it and let a wondering look creep across his seamed face.

"Why, I believe that plaguey pain in my foot is done faded right away," he declared in awed tones. "I'm cured! Praise be to God! Hallelujah!"

Maybe Briggs laid it on a little thick, but the crowd responded with more than good-humored hooting and badinage. They also bought numerous bottles of Colonel Ruddy's wares, pretty well depleting his stock.

Aussie gave sly nudges to the ribs of Lazlo and Hutch, who stood on either side of him. "Ain't 'e the silver-tongued old snake-oil artist, though! I'll lay yer any odds that medicine of his is 'arf straight alcohol. But it'll get a chap feeling 'is oats for a spell, and no mistake."

"You reckon that's what it done for old Briggs?" Hutch asked.

" 'Ell no, guv. Briggsy is just a shill. Like enough the colonel slipped 'im a few bob in advance. More like yet, 'e slipped 'im a bottle full of just 'is basic ingredient. Briggsy was wobbling a bit on 'is pins before 'e took the blinkin' elixir, I noticed."

"I think so," said Lazlo. "Maybe then, this Colonel Ruddy

also has some tricks up his sleeve for the wrestling and shooting contests . . . eh?"

Aussie laughed quietly. "You can bet your bonnet on it, chum. You got to 'and it to 'im. He's a rum customer, 'e is! All the same, gents, I'm of the opinion we can 'oist the old poop from 'is own blinkin' petard. Think I got 'is game sized up proper. Just you wait."

* * *

The wrestling competition was held on a scuffed level of ground, with the colonel officiating. But he gave the business a semblance of fairness by letting the crowd nominate the referee, an elderly miner that everyone trusted. Then he introduced, with many verbal flourishes, the two strong men of his show who would take on all comers.

A pair of young men came bounding out of a wagon, and they were something to see. They were clad alike in jaguar-hide breechclouts and nothing else. Their thews swelled and rippled to their exaggerated swaggers as they advanced to the center of the ring. Colonel Ruddy had announced them as "those famous Italian wrestlers, the marvels of two continents —the Altrocchi twins, Roberto and Raphael!"

But while their similarly swarthy looks might pass for Italian, they obviously weren't twins. Brothers no doubt, thought Lazlo, but not twins. Roberto was bigger and more massively muscled than Raphael.

Roberto, living up to the colonel's promise of "a remarkable display of sheer might," raised on high an iron bar he was carrying. With a seemingly contemptuous ease, he bent the bar to a right angle and tossed it aside.

That was impressive. So was Colonel Ruddy's offer to ten-to-one odds on either "twin." He would pay a dollar to every dime if any man in the crowd could defeat either of his strong men.

Roberto would be the first to stand forth against all comers. He strutted up and down, flexing his great thews.

"Hell, I'll take them odds!" yelled a big young miner. "By grab, I'll dump that dago on his dumb ass or my name ain't Brawlin' Billy Griswold!"

A burst of cheers from the crowd.

Brawlin' Billy stood a full head taller than Roberto Altrocchi and was a sight heftier. All the same, the betting ran heavy against Billy. The crowd wasn't about to take even highly tempting odds against any man who could bend an iron bar so readily.

Griswold peeled off his jacket and shirt, his shoes and socks, to even things up somewhat against his breechclouted, barefoot opponent. Brawlin' Billy was a formidable hulk of a man, all right. But his musculature didn't have the swelling, iron-hard look of Roberto's.

Nevertheless Brawlin' Billy won the match handily. He pinned his opponent in two out of three grunting, straining falls. The crowd groaned and cheered, and paid or collected their money. As many had laid bets among themselves as had taken up Colonel Ruddy's offer.

Grinning gleefully, Aussie beckoned his two companions to one side.

"Well, chums, it went like I told yer it would. That dago chap threw the match for certain."

Hutch scratched his curly head, scowling. "You reckon that's so?"

"Can it be?" Lazlo said doubtfully. "I think this has cost the colonel a pretty penny."

"'E 'ad 'is man throw it, you can place bottom bob on it," insisted Aussie. "That's the 'ole game, don't yer see? 'Ere, take a look at this. I sneaked it off the ground when nobody was looking . . ."

He slipped an object from beneath his coat, holding it closely between Lazlo and Hutch for their examination. It was the bent iron bar that Roberto had cast aside. "See them marks where it's been worked on with a file . . . 'ere and 'ere? And the cuts 'idden with wax and boot blacking. Took a strong man to bend 'er, all right. But not near as strong as that guinea was letting on."

Hutch shook his head, mystified. "I don't savvy this here a-tall. If that Roberto was in a way to lose, how come the colonel offered odds like he give on him?"

"Why guv, 'e knew there wasn't many 'ud take 'im up on that bet. 'E was casting bread unto the waters, in a manner of speaking. 'E means to get it back manyfold, if yer follow me. I'll tell yer 'ow, chums. 'Ark to me close, now . . ."

Aussie's explanation was hasty but thorough.

The three of them pushed their way to the front of the throng. Colonel Ruddy was offering to cover all bets on his second wrestler, whom he would put against any comer.

Hutch bellied forward, grinning. "Looks like easy money," he declared loudly. "I'll take it. I'll take that Eye-talian to a fare-thee-well too."

Colonel Ruddy took in Hutch's considerable bulk with narrowed eyes. Then he laughed, smoothing his goatee with a finger. His big teeth gleamed above it. "You're on, my friend. Wagers, anyone? Same odds as before."

This time around, the colonel had a mob of takers.

Hutch and Raphael squared off on the circle of packed ground, Hutch barefoot and stripped to the waist. There was plenty of solid muscle under Hutch's blubber, and it was pretty hard-looking blubber at that. He moved with an easy-footed, unexpected grace.

Meantime Aussie was circulating busily through the crowd, laying bets with everyone he could corner, including the colonel. Now he slipped back to Lazlo's side.

"I got every cent riding on our friend," he reported. "We're going to make a killing, chum."

"You think," said Lazlo.

"I been telling yer, I feel it in my bones. There they go, now."

The two brawny antagonists began to circle one another. Both were panther-quick, and Hutch's great size seemed to offset the cable-muscled trimness of his opponent.

The way Aussie had explained it, Brawlin' Billy's defeat of the bigger Altrocchi brother had been a setup to lure the suckers in. The crowd would now be certain to bet heavily against the smaller brother, confident that one of their own could take him even more easily. But Raphael, thought Aussie, was no doubt the really accomplished wrestler of the two. No doubt too that he intended to fetch the crowd a surprise by pinning their man with comparative ease.

Only it wasn't going to be easy. Hutch's mighty heft, taken by itself, would ensure that. Moreover he'd wrestled in a number of camptown dogfalls. Several times, he had put down Brawlin' Billy Griswold himself. Aussie was gambling that Hutch could do the same to Raphael.

He did too.

It was exactly as the previous match had gone, except that it went on a lot longer. Both men were pouring sweat before Hutch won the first fall. They went back at it with an even more ferocious, jaw-locked energy, and this time Raphael won the fall. The third round must have dragged on for nearly a half-hour before Hutch slammed his adversary's shoulders to the ground.

The crowd went wild. Bets were collected—and paid.

Colonel Ruddy effected to pay off cheerfully. But there was a hard burn of blood in his cheeks, and his smile was teeth-clenched. He was a man who noticed things. More than once his gaze sought out Hutch and Aussie with a cold knowledge.

"We dropped some sand in 'is nibs's gear box for certain," Aussie said with a wolfish pleasure. "Let's toss in a little more, gents, what d'ye say?"

CHAPTER 3

The colonel introduced his next attraction as "Sureshot Stell," a lady whom he insisted could shoot rings around even that paragon of riflewomen, Mrs. Annie Oakley Butler.

The crowd hooted a little at this. But they quieted down a bit when the lady in question made her appearance from one of the wagons.

Sureshot Stell looked keen-eyed and competent. After the fashion of Calamity Jane and other celebrated women of the camps, she wore men's clothing, complete with cowboy boots and a horsethief hat. She might have been in her midtwenties. She was on the tall and wiry side but sturdy too, and her dark hair was cut mannishly short. For all that, oddly enough, she wasn't unfeminine.

Most important, Lazlo observed, she carried a rifle as if she'd been born with one in her hand.

"Watch 'er now, chum," Aussie murmured. "Let 'er use 'erself up on a few of these yokels as fancy 'emselves marksmen. Then, you trots out your stuff. But watch 'er close the while."

Lazlo nodded. He was feeling a little dizzy and sickish once more. The pick-me-ups he'd taken had worn off. The sun was quite hot now, baking through his wreck of a hat into his throbbing head.

Sureshot Stell appeared very confident as she sauntered out to the bare stretch of ground, but it didn't really make any difference. A whole lot of men tended to be unshakably vain about their shooting ability, even when they didn't possess any. Most of them believed they could shade any woman who ever lived at any damned pastime under the sun that was a traditionally masculine one.

That, ran Lazlo's shrewd guess, would be part of Sureshot Stell's advantage. Betting went heavily against her as her first opponent, an excessively cocky miner, strutted out to take his place beside her.

The rules, as the colonel loudly declaimed them, were simple. Shooters could use either a rifle or a pistol. Glass balls would be tossed up to serve as targets, and the sharpshooters would try to shatter them before they hit the ground. Each person was allowed only one shot per ball before it landed. After twenty throws (provided that both contestants "made the mark"), "time" would be called for five minutes in order to let the contestants rest and give their weapons a little while to cool off. Then another round would commence. Glass balls, the colonel added, were used as targets because the referee could always tell at a glance if one had been hit. Even "chipping" one with a bullet would count as a hit. The first contestant to miss a shot completely would lose the match. Raphael Altrocchi would pitch up the glass orbs for Stell; the opponent could pick his own ball tosser. Ruddy urged the crowd to give the adversaries plenty of room.

The young miner stayed up with Stell for a toss of six balls. Then he missed. A groan ran through the crowd.

She was good, Lazlo thought. Sureshot Stell was very good.

She was a machine of a woman, calmly and smoothly levering fresh loads into the breech of her Henry .44 rifle, ejecting the spent rimfire shells in a litter around her booted feet. Lazlo watched her with a concentration that made him momentarily forget his growing sickness. He had more than a sneaking conviction that this lady could keep up her performance for a long time yet and never miss a shot.

Her next opponent, using a Colt .45 revolver, knocked out eight balls before dropping one. The third man missed his target on the third throw.

The crowd was starting to grumble. An impression that they had been "had" was starting to percolate into their collective consciousness. But then, as they further commenced to assume, it was likely that Sureshot Stell's eye or arm would begin to tire before too long. After all, she was only a woman.

Now the insistent ache in Lazlo's head was spreading behind his eyeballs. Nervous sweat broke on his temples; he rubbed them with his fingertips. He looked at one of his hands; it was shaking. God, how was he going to manage in this condition?

Even if he weren't on the bad end of a monumental hangover, he wondered how he would fare against this woman. True, he had won a few shooting competitions in the camp, including some like this one—firing at inanimate objects that someone threw into the air.

Lazlo had never begun to burn powder with any idea of gaining an inordinate skill. He had acquired his Winchester repeating rifle several years ago when he'd started to follow the lonely trails in search of gold. It had seemed a common-sense provision—that was all—for his own protection and for securing meat.

But he'd discovered an unexpected affinity for the weapon. He would practice with it on all kinds of targets: bottles, tin cans, twigs, pine cones, wood chips, pebbles. It was fun to do and gave him a release from work and tension. So he had become proficient.

Lazlo knew he was good. But just how good? Even at his best, what sort of show would he stand against a sharpshooter of Stell's caliber?

Aussie was eyeing him with a touch of concern. "Bit under the weather, eh, sport?"

"Yes. I am afraid so."

Aussie dipped into his pocket and produced a flask. "To go up against this lady, you'll need a steady 'and. Take a swig. This 'ere is none of your camptown swill. Cognac, it is, and nothing but the best."

Lazlo uncapped the flask and took a pull. The liquor had a smooth dark glow that warmed him evenly from tongue to belly.

"Take another," said Aussie and grinned. "I kind of thought yer'd be needing it. That's enough now. Trot yourself out there and throw down your gauge. 'Utch, 'ow about you toss up the balls for 'im?"

Hutch eyed the flask as Lazlo passed it back. He swiped the

back of a hairy fist across his mouth. "Sure thing. Reckon my hand could use a mite of steadying too . . ."

"All right, but not too bleedin' much," Aussie cautioned as he handed over the flask. "Our chum 'ere'll be needing a bit more later on, or I miss my guess."

A ripple of excitement went through the crowd as Lazlo Kusik stepped out to offer his challenge to Sureshot Stell.

The camp knew him as a loner who rarely sought the company of his fellow miners. But on the convivial occasions he'd attended, when any test of prowess with a rifle was offered, he'd shot rings around all his opponents. This had occurred only three times since Lazlo's arrival in Bozetown, yet in a small, gossipy camp it had been enough to cinch his reputation as a marksman.

At just this moment, Lazlo was feeling far from sure of himself.

The cognac had steadied his nerves and hands, but it had also left him in a slight, pleasant alcoholic haze that he feared might prove fatal to his eye and aim. Just a hair's breadth of timing could make all the difference when you were firing at a thrown object.

Also he had never shot at glass balls. These appeared to be about two inches in diameter; he'd knocked down much smaller objects, such as two-bit pieces. But he'd noted the harsh glint of sun on the flung balls, which might trick even an experienced eye. A gust of wind might affect a ball's natural arc. He wondered if these factors hadn't disconcerted the previous shooters.

Except for Sureshot Stell. She would know exactly how to allow for such vagaries.

She gave him a brief, speculative glance of her ice-gray eyes as he stepped out to the trampled stretch of ground and took his place about ten feet to her left. Her cool inspection of him showed only a bored interest, but she hadn't missed the crowd's stir of reaction.

This close to her, Lazlo could take a better look at her rifle. He was sure it was a specially crafted piece, probably hand-worked. Lightweight, no doubt, and of a hairfine accuracy. The ordinary Henry .44 repeating rifle was a heavy weapon and was likely to tire the arms of even a strong man after a period of rapidly lifting and firing it.

Sureshot Stell was a real professional. She had every reason to be confident.

I think she has got all her bases covered, Lazlo thought with bleak humor. He liked that phrase derived from the ingenious game of baseball to which, at one convivial gathering, some miners had introduced him.

Now his senses felt honed to an edge; all details seemed crisp and sharp in his vision. That was the alcohol working, and he did not trust it, but he trusted the wily saloonkeeper. Aussie, who was again busily circulating and laying bets among the crowd, would gauge things like that to a fine degree.

Hutch swaggered out to the bucketful of glass balls that one of the Altrocchis had set in place for Lazlo. He picked one up and examined it, then gave Lazlo a broad wink.

"Go to 'er, little pard," he said loudly. "We're counting on you to whup the pants off her!"

His own remark struck Hutch—and some of the onlookers —as exceedingly hilarious. He gave a whoop and whipped his hat off, slapping it against his thigh.

Sureshot Stell turned a cool look on him. She said calmly, "I reckon you didn't mean nothing special by that, now did you, Slim?"

Hutch eyed the rifle she held so competently and let his vast grin relax to a polite smirk. "Not a thing under the sun, ma'am, and that's God's truth."

As he had before, the old miner who'd been nominated referee checked out the buckets of glass balls that were allotted to each contestant. He did this by spilling them all on the ground, examining each ball in turn and returning it to its bucket. There were twenty-five balls to a bucket, more than enough for a full round of firing.

At a word—"Throw!"—from the referee, the ball tossers sent a pair of glass spheres winging against the sky.

Lazlo's Winchester swung smoothly to match the climb of the ball. When it hung poised at the peak of its arc, he fired.

Although he blinked against an unexpected flash of sunlight on the orb, it dissolved in a shower of kaleidoscopic shards.

A perfect hit. The crowd gave him a mild hand of applause.

Sureshot Stell had made her score too. But something had struck Lazlo as being a bit off-center.

Glancing at Stell now, he said politely, "I would like to call time if it is all right."

"You can't do that, young fellow," Colonel Ruddy said sternly. "No time will be called till this round is over."

"But you would not want your shooter to have an unfair advantage?"

"*What's* unfair?" Stell demanded with a touch of heat. "You better make that clear, Jack."

"There is no offense meant."

Lazlo walked over to her and stood in back of her, sighting over her shoulder. "The sun hits on my targets as it cannot on yours, I think. Where you are standing, that big tree over yonder cuts off the sunlight."

Stell turned enough to let her eyes lock his in a chill meeting. She was as tall as he and they were, eye to eye.

Then she shrugged. "All right, Jack. You can stand any place you damn well fancy. Now. Are you happy?"

"Thank you."

A glint of amusement touched her stare. She was not a pretty woman; "pretty" was too soft a term to apply to Sureshot Stell. But she was a damned handsome woman. And of course she'd been well aware of the advantage she had taken.

Lazlo moved to a fresh position where the same tree shadow would cover his throws. He motioned Hutch to readjust his own position; then he and Stell took their stances again.

Once more two balls were thrown up; both were shattered to pieces.

Lazlo's doubts began to ease. This was not so bad after all, he thought as he levered his Winchester for the third throw. All you had to do was to keep topmost in your mind that you were not shooting to beat anyone, you were shooting only to hit a glass ball. Only that.

It was not nearly so simple, but if you made yourself think that it was, you would be all right. That way you could shut out all thought of personalities, and a glass ball was only a glass ball.

He did not look directly at Stell again. He fixed all his thoughts on the rhythm of his shooting. Lever. Lift. Aim. Fire. Tinkle and splatter of glass. Deafening gun roar that slammed against his ears over and over.

Lazlo felt sweat crawl down his ribs. His shoulder was a little numb from absorbing the recoil of his weapon so many times in quick succession. He did not pause except to reload his magazine. His concentration was so intense that the repetition of his own effort was becoming a kind of punishing deadly ritual.

One that, it seemed, might go on forever.

When time was called, he blinked and lowered his rifle, hardly aware of the noisy applause that swept through the crowd. His eyes met Stell's again. Her face showed nothing, but a sheen of sweat dampened her upper lip.

Lazlo walked to where Aussie was waiting at the edge of the throng.

"You're doing wondrous fine, chum!" the little saloon man greeted him. "I got all the wagers laid. If yer can outlast that blinkin' wench, the three of us'll divide a smart piece of money among us."

Hutch joined them, grinning hugely. "By grab, I think we got that pants-proud filly on the run! What d'you think, little pard?"

"I don't know. I was not watching so close." Lazlo set his hands to his ears. "The noise of the guns . . . I think it is starting to rattle my brain."

"Christ!" Aussie was instantly contrite. "I must of left *my* bloomin' brains in storage today. Should of 'ad yer plug yer ears against the concussion. It gets to affecting a body something fierce after a good spell of steady shooting . . ."

As he spoke, Aussie took a tattered bandanna out of his pocket. He tore off a couple of its ragged edges and balled each one into small wads between his fingers. "There y'are, chum . . . a pair of earplugs that will serve to a fare-thee-well. 'Ow're yer feeling otherwise?"

"I think all right."

"Good. 'Ere now." Aussie got out the cognac flask, took a swallow from it, and shoved it at Lazlo. "Just a little 'un, mind you. Won't 'urt yer none, and I've a 'unch it'll 'it the old spot just right."

It hit the spot exactly right.

Lazlo took his drink and handed the flask to Hutch. His gaze sought Sureshot Stell, who was conferring with Colonel Ruddy a little distance away. The colonel didn't look at all happy. He stood with fists braced on his hips; he was tight-lipped when his bearded jaw wasn't chopping out a rush of hard-clipped words.

Lazlo wondered if Ruddy's irritation stemmed from Stell's having given in so easily to Lazlo's objection. Stell appeared to be dryly amused, not at all disconcerted by whatever the colonel was saying.

Ruddy pulled out his watch and gazed at it. The last seconds ticked off, and the five-minute break was up. The contestants took their places again.

Again the *crack-crack* of the rifles. Bits of disintegrating glass catching twinkles of light as they fell to the ground. The devouring rhythm that numbed a man's mind against everything else.

At first, with his hearing somewhat muffled, Lazlo had an easier time of it. But he could feel a tender ache creeping more quickly now through his arms and shoulders. A lighter gun might have stood him in good stead, for he sensed—without taking a direct look at Sureshot Stell—that she was feeling the strain too. She had the advantage of experience, but quite probably she hadn't often had to face an opponent who could hold out against her so long.

Forget her. Fix on those flying balls of glass—nothing else. Lever. Lift. Aim. Fire . . .

The steady ache spread into the upper muscles of Lazlo's trunk. His arms began to feel heavy, the Winchester even heavier. A red throbbing touched the edges of his vision. He was literally pouring sweat. Fearing it might run into his eyes, he kept swiping a sleeve across his brow. Above all, he must keep his eyes clear.

Lever. Lift. Aim. Fire!

On the fourteenth throw, the crowd let out an involuntary groan.

That riffle of reaction gave Lazlo a start. Till now, during this round, the audience had been silent and intent, transfixed by the duel.

Lazlo had exploded his glass ball.

Glancing toward Sureshot Stell now, he saw the truth in her face even before his glance shuttled to the last sphere that Raphael had thrown. It lay untouched on the scuffed turf less than ten yards away.

Sureshot Stell had missed her shot.

Then Aussie was pounding him on the back, shouting triumphantly, "Yer done it, chum! Yer done it! We've made a bleedin' score, we 'ave!" At the same time, Hutch's massive fist was enclosing his hand in a crushing grip.

Lazlo said, "Just a minute, is that all right with you?" and pulled away from both of them.

He went over to Sureshot Stell, who was calmly inspecting the mechanism of her rifle. Now her face showed only a stony indifference, but she was pale around the lips.

"Ain't nobody ever outshot me in three years of this," she said quietly. "You are some shuckins with that piece, mister."

Lazlo hesitated. He did not know what he wanted to say. Finally he said simply, "I am sorry."

"Not half as sorry as I be," Sureshot Stell said curtly. She brushed past him, heading for one of the wagons.

Looking past her, Lazlo's glance crossed Colonel Laban Ruddy's. The colonel was gazing straight at him, and in his look there was something that went beyond mere irritation. Something like a flicker of venomous fury . . .

CHAPTER 4

Laban Ruddy's hand shook as he laid out a game of solitaire on the small deal table. A lamp with a low-burning flame and a half-empty bottle of whiskey also occupied the table's scarred top. Reaching unsteadily for the glass at his elbow, Laban knocked it over and flooded his cards with whiskey.

"Shit!" Laban exploded. He spat out the shred of cheroot clamped between his jaws, and then sent the glass and the soaked cards flying with a furious sweep of his arm.

"Them's my sentiments exactly," said Sureshot Stell.

Laban swung his head toward the open door of his wagon, glaring at her. Stell was standing just outside, thumbs hooked in the belt loops of her pants, grinning a little.

"What the hell, Pa. You can't expect to rake in the pot every deal. So we took it in the neck once."

Laban felt his usual nudge of distaste at Stell's crude speech, but it was only a weary drunken flicker. He'd been listening to it for too many years to be much affected anymore. Besides he knew she swore and otherwise acted like a man largely to irritate him.

"'Got it in the neck,'" he echoed bitterly. "What we are, is cleaned out, girl. Those men pulled a setup, and we have gotten taken proper."

"Well, that's fair enough, ain't it?" Stell said promptly. "We done our share of taking, God knows. Look, Pa, that foreign man beat me fair and square. And the big fellow took Bije the same way."

"Haven't you a shred of pride?" Laban asked coldly. "I'd think you'd be up in arms. Whipped on your own grounds by a lowdown hunky miner!"

Stell lifted one shoulder in a philosophical shrug. "I felt a mite peeved at first. But hell, he shaded me by a little, that's all. Today he did. 'Nother day, I might of won. That's how it is with 'most any good shootist. Forget it, Pa. There's other camps. We'll make up our losses next place we come to."

Laban said grimly, "That's a lot of money to drop at one shot." Absently he bent over and picked up a few of the wet cards, then flung them down with an angry oath.

"Such a way to talk," Stell said innocently.

Making a thin effort to conceal his irritation, he said, "How is your sister doing?"

"Myra Mae is taking a nap in our wagon." She shook her head. "Pa, you hadn't ought to take her on the road anymore. She ain't well."

"Hogwash," the colonel said shortly. "Myra Mae is only sixteen and healthy as a horse. Basically she is, I mean. Wager it's just a case of feminine 'blues.' This has been a long stint for all of us, but we'll be packing off to winter quarters soon . . ."

"When?"

Laban frowned at the brusqueness of her query. "When I say so. Go on, now. Go shoot up something with that damned rifle of yours, why don't you? Apparently you could use a little practice."

Stell gave a good-natured hoot of derision.

She said, "Yeah, more than you need with that damned bottle," then turned and sauntered away.

Laban Ruddy dug out a fresh cheroot, bit off the end, and savagely spat it out. Then he sat staring at the tabletop, the cheroot cold between his fingers.

Damn that Australian Duck! He was a sharper for certain—the colonel always knew another of the breed at a glance—and he must have cleaned up on today's heavy betting, collecting from Laban himself and from a number of affluent betters in the crowd. And of course he'd have split his winnings with the other two. Laban hadn't missed how chummy Aussie had been with both the hunky sharpshooter and the big wrestler.

Won fair and square, had they? Well, maybe they had. Even

so, Laban had a bitter conviction that he'd been taken. He felt outraged by the mere thought that the Duck had somehow outsmarted him.

Nobody, goddammit, did that to Laban Ruddy!

For a full hour, Laban had been brooding on the matter over a bottle. For several years, during the warmer seasons, he and the remaining members of his family—two daughters and two nephews—had made a comfortable living without too much effort, traveling from one frontier camp to the next and putting on their show. It worked out pretty well, with Myra Mae's youthful concupiscence providing the come-on, followed by his own slick medicine spiel, his nephews' wrestling act, and Stell's sharpshooting. Usually they'd clear enough to live high off the hog at their leisure, for the five or six months of each year when they'd "winter" anywhere from New Orleans to San Francisco.

It was a pleasant way of life, one made to order for an ex–circus barker who'd found he could do better with an itinerant medicine show (with side attractions) than he ever had shouting himself hoarse in Barnum and Bailey's sawdust ring. And he was his own boss. Colonel Laban Ruddy had fallen into a pleasurable rut from which—after a few contented seasons of it—he had no intention of being dislocated.

But today had thrust a shocking reversal on all his expectations. He and the kids had made a real killing this season. They would have gone into "winter quarters" with so much loot that he could have afforded to bank quite a piece of it away . . . against his declining years.

Today Laban Ruddy had recklessly bet nearly every cent he'd made this season on the usual course of yokel-rooking which he followed. And he'd lost damned near all of it on a couple of unexpected upsets: two defeats of his performers within the space of a couple hours.

That damned Australian was to blame. And he had all those winnings, he and his two cohorts. While Laban and his family would face a long, dismal winter of scrabbling and minching just to make it through . . . till they could get on the road again next spring.

Laban retrieved his unbroken glass from the floor, filled it to the brim with whiskey, and gulped it down.

Make up their losses at the next camp? Not a chance! It would take another whole season, and a damned lucky one at that, to approach what they had earned this year. With the high-country winter closing down, soon to shut off the mountain trails, he hadn't planned on extending the present circuit to more than another camp or two.

Laban Ruddy's fist clenched around the empty glass. *Well, by God, we'll see.* His decision was made. He swayed to his feet and moved unsteadily to the door, peering rheumily out.

The setting sun laid a pearly glow over the autumn-brown drabness of Humbug Flat. The three wagons were drawn up to form the partial sides of a triangle with its corners open. One wagon was Laban's own; another housed his daughters. His nephews and Robert Topbear—who was no Ojibway or a chief's son, only a Creek-Cherokee outcast—occupied the third. A supper fire had been started in the center of the triangle.

The dark, stocky pair of brothers known to patrons of the medicine circus as "Roberto and Raphael Altrocchi" were squatting on their haunches over a checkerboard laid out on a flat rock. Both were staring at the board, scowling, arms folded on their knees.

"Pretty intellectual game for you boys, isn't it?" Laban said with a drunken, sardonic leer. "Get in here, both of you. I want to talk to you."

Obediently, Abraham and Abijah Willet got to their feet and tramped over to the wagon. Laban stepped aside to let them climb inside, then closed the door behind them. The girls were in their wagon and "Wa-nit-ka-we-bo" would be sleeping off a head of booze in his. Laban just wanted to be sure that neither of the girls overheard this conversation.

Laban slumped back into the only chair and poured himself a drink. Ab and Bije squatted down facing him, glancing incuriously around their uncle's cramped and sparsely furnished quarters, its walls papered with faded posters from Laban's cir-

cus days. Their muscles bulged thickly against the rough shirts
and trousers they now wore.

Studying their dull faces through his alcoholic blur, Laban
thought: *God, if these two could scrape up even half a brain
between them, they'd have about a quarter of what I have dead
sober.*

Laban sometimes wondered why that was. The boys'
mother, his own departed sister, had been a bright girl of some
accomplishments, and Jim Willet, the glib traveling man she'd
wed, had been no slouch in the mental department either. But
this pair . . . ! If there weren't old Uncle Laban to watch out
for them, God knew what would become of 'em.

Important thing was, Ab and Bije were proficient at just
about anything that required physical action. They took orders
well, and once you dunned into their heads what was expected
of them, you could depend on them to do a proper job of it.

Laban leaned back in his chair, crossing his legs. "Boys," he
said mildly, "it will be necessary to resuscitate our resources
before proceeding on our way."

They gazed at him unblinkingly for some moments. Then
Bije, slightly smaller than his brother, younger by a year, and
brighter by a hair's breadth, knitted his brows. "What's that
there resusci-mabobble mean, Uncle Labe?"

"It means," Laban said in a kindly way, "that we have been
done out of a peck of money today, and I have a notion how
we can get back quite a lot of it. Now, you two flaming wits
pay attention to what I tell you. I don't want to have to repeat
it more than four or five times."

*   *   *

After a delighted Aussie divided his winnings among Lazlo,
Hutch, and himself, the three of them separated. Aussie returned to his saloon, Hutch set out to "make the rounds" of
every drinking dive in Bozetown, and Lazlo headed for the
local livery barn to see what kind of a deal he could wangle
for a wagon. He also bought a trustworthy mule named Matilda to hitch in tandem with his mule Prunes.

The wagon he chose was a sturdy-looking Studebaker that
had seen some use, having served the U.S. Cavalry for several

years as a supply vehicle. Lazlo considered it all the better for that, since now the wagon would be nicely "seasoned"; any defects would have shown up before now. Old Gaffer, the livery owner who told him its brief history, had a reputation for fair dealing. And a good solid wagon was a key factor in Lazlo's plan.

From there he went to the local sawmill, where he purchased a dozen fresh-cut pine planks, each about ten feet long and an inch thick, along with several stout two-by-fours. Loading these in the wagon, he made a final stop at the mercantile store. Here he bought a gallon of paint, a paintbrush, a saw and hammer, and a sack of nails.

With some food supplies added to the load, he was starting out of town when Hutch Prouter came lurching out of a saloon. Spotting Lazlo, he bawled, "Hey, little pard! You wasn't fixing to depart 'thout hoisting a victory glass 'ith ole Hutch, now was you?"

Feeling he couldn't flatly refuse without giving a nudge to any suspicions Hutch might harbor, Lazlo joined him for a couple of drinks. Afterward he was adamant about not repeating last night's drunken tear but gave in to Hutch's insistence that they have supper together at the China Cafe.

"Yessir, little pard . . ." Hutch rambled along between mouthfuls as he tore apart and devoured a roast canvasback duck. "Ain't but one thing to do with money when a man has it. That's spend it."

Lazlo said easily, "Maybe you are right," as he methodically cut and chewed and swallowed mouthfuls of a thick steak. It wasn't a bad cut of meat for gold-camp fare . . . even at gold-camp prices.

Hutch mopped up the last gravy on his plate with a wad of bread and wolfed it down. He gave a mighty belch of satisfaction, wiping his greasy paws on his pants. "Betcher ass. Well . . . looks like you will be pulling out o' here with a mite o' change in your pockets after all, hey?"

Lazlo nodded. "It was a good day. Even divided between us three, it comes to a good piece of money for each."

"Yeah, middlin'." Hutch patted his paunch and glanced over

his shoulder toward the waitress. "Hey, sister! More coffee over here." His veiled glance grazed over Lazlo's face. "But they's plenty loot bigger'n that waiting in them hills . . . if a man could strike it."

Lazlo smiled faintly. "That is the little problem, eh? *If.*"

"Well, a fella most always can't tell. Maybe if you was to hang on for another year . . ."

"I do not think so. Soon the snow and cold will close up the mountains. Now will be a good time to pull out. One can do better with a long winter than stick it out in this place."

"Could be," Hutch said agreeably. "'Pends what kind o' prospects a man has got. Where you be heading to, Laz?"

"Saba City. I have a little color in my poke. Not much, but I can get cash for it at the assay office here. With what I have won today, I will have enough to get by for a little time. I have not thought what I will do next. But there is always something."

"Sure is, if a man has got wits in his head and guts in his belly. Always something . . . yes sirree." Hutch picked his teeth with a splinter of duck bone. His eyes, now focused on a point above Lazlo's head, held a musing and faraway look. "Y' know, though, be a dandy thing if a fella could pack out o' these digs with more'n a passel of busted hopes in his possible sack. That Saba City'd be some place to start a-spending it, I tell you."

His gaze drifted idly back to Lazlo.

"Sure." Lazlo reached for his refilled mug of coffee. "It would be a fine thing."

He wasn't deceived by Hutch's casual probing. Somehow in an unrecalled slip of the tongue, he must have given away at least a triumphant hint of his discovery during last night's long libations. Enough to put an edge on Hutch's watchful cupidity.

And now Hutch was slyly digging, skirting around the central question but always circling back to it and going out of his way to look sleepily unconcerned about it. His approach, however, was too slyly circumspect to convince anyone. If a man weren't expecting anything of the sort, he might easily be taken in by Hutch's guileless manner. But Lazlo, riding a fine blade of wariness these many weeks, was too jumpy and nerve-knotted to be caught off guard. Right now, if one of the Lord's angels were to confront Lazlo Kusik in all its glory, it would be met by a stony suspicion. He did his best to be casual and pleasant with Hutch and to show nothing else at all.

They left the cafe. By now the swift mountain twilight had flushed out of the sky; it was pitch-dark. Hutch belched and rubbed his vast belly. "Sure you don't want to take on another bumper o' tanglefoot?"

"I had enough last night. I would think you had too."

Hutch laughed, clapping a hand on Lazlo's shoulder. "Warn't it the truth! But I ain't taken on near enough today, heh-heh. When you figure on pulling out for Saba City?"

"I don't know. Maybe the day after tomorrow."

"Well, I will drop by your digs afore then. Pleasant dreams, little pard."

Hutch lumbered off toward the nearest saloon.

Lazlo's new wagon stood at the tie rail, his team of mules hitched to the tailgate so they could forage on some hay stowed in the wagon bed. He watered them at a nearby trough and hitched them up. Then he headed south out of town.

The muddy mire of a wagon road that bisected the camp petered out in a twisting lane below the town. It followed the west bank of the Mad Mule River, an old game and Indian trail now used solely by the few prospectors who had staked claim along the lower reaches of the river. A quarter moon relieved some of the darkness; a cool wind brushed off the western peaks. Lazlo shivered, wishing that he had his Mackinaw coat along.

After a while, the trail swung away from the river, dipping past the mouth of Trevo Pass. This broad and brush-clogged cleft in the western ramparts of the Elk Mountains was sometimes used by men on foot as a shortcut across the mountains. Lazlo had been over it quite a few times himself. But no wagon had ever tried to negotiate that same rough and rambling trail. A little distance east of the pass lay Hutch Prouter's riverside camp and claim, hidden from the road by trees.

The wagon careened and jolted over the pitted trail. Now it

was narrowing to a slender trace that ran between the river-bank on one side and a steep, pine-mantled ridge on the other. The trail was barely wide enough to accommodate the wagon, and Lazlo slowed and guided the mules across it with care. A thin glare of moonlight sent a rippling sheen across the river, but the high pitch of slope and the looming pines made deep pools of shadow that obscured most details of what was around him.

Lazlo had been over this trail often enough to have a pretty accurate idea of the worst bumps and turnings. Even so, at one point he halted the wagon in order to give a little thought to what lay just ahead of him.

Pulling up the team caused the rattle of hooves and harness to ebb suddenly into silence. In that moment Lazlo heard something else: a sound that pulled him alert right away, that didn't belong to the hushed current of river on his left or to the sough of wind through the pines on his right.

It was a light thud of running feet on the trail behind him. And it ceased just moments after he reined in the mules.

Someone . . . following close on his back and catching up fast. No, more than one. At least two of them for sure. He was being stalked in the darkness . . .

Lazlo's rifle was out of easy reach, wedged among the supplies in the wagon bed. Easily, making no sudden moves, he loosened the Bowie knife in its sheath at his hip. He did not look around. The stalkers were close to the ground; he was skylined on the seat. Any obvious move on his part would be spotted. If he glanced backward, he was sure he would see only impenetrable shadow.

He clucked to the team and gave the reins a shake, and the mules slogged forward. But now Lazlo kept his head tipped a little to his left . . . enough to let the tail of his eye register any hint of movement it picked up toward his back.

The creak of wagon and harness, the slow clop of hooves covered any other sound. But the edge of his vision picked up a quick change in the flow of shadows to his left.

The running figure was almost alongside him, a clublike object raised in its fist. In the same instant, Lazlo yanked his

Bowie knife from its leather sheath and rolled sideways off the seat, away from the club wielder. He hit the ground catlike on his feet and then wheeled around at once, confronting exactly what he'd expected: the shadowy hulk of the second assailant.

This one, too, carried a truncheon of some kind. He swung it savagely at Lazlo's head. Lazlo ducked and felt his hat carried away by the aborted blow, and then he wove under the man's guard and whipped up his Bowie in a quick vicious thrust at the indistinct form.

The knife went between the body and arm of his adversary but didn't entirely miss. Lazlo heard a startled grunt of pain as the blade ripped through cloth and then flesh.

Briefly the other attacker was cut off by the wagon. Already, though, he had leaped to the seat and was scrambling across it. Crouching just above Lazlo, he swung at the latter's head. Lazlo gave a sidelong twist that saved his skull, but the club slammed his shoulder with an impact that numbed his whole right arm.

Lazlo melted to the ground, switching the Bowie to his left hand as he flung himself under the wagon to escape a second swiping blow by the man he'd cut. The one on the seat leaped down in the same instant that Lazlo squirmed around on his belly, lightning-fast. Lazlo took a sweeping awkward slash at the fellow's leg.

This time his blade struck through boot leather and into the flesh and bone of an ankle. The man screamed and stumbled away, then fell to his hands and knees. Lazlo rolled over twice, away from both assailants, and came out on the other side of the wagon.

Both men were cursing furiously as Lazlo swung to his feet and threw an arm across the wagon's sideboard. At once, by instinct, his hand closed on the stock of his Winchester. He dragged it free of the load and levered it once sharply.

The curses broke off. Both assailants took to their heels, plunging away down the trail—one of them supporting his limping companion. Lazlo had a couple of fleeting glimpses of the men before the shadows swallowed them. He fired a little over their heads, then levered his rifle and fired again.

The running sounds died away, fading off among the shot echoes.

Lazlo stood for a long moment, listening, the wind cool on his sweating face. The hurt of his right shoulder became less intolerable as he gently massaged it. The thumping of his heart slowed. He retrieved his hat and swung back up to the wagon's high seat, gathering up the reins. Both mules had come to a stop and had stood placidly through the brief fracas.

He gave them each a word or two of commendation, knowing it would make no difference. An earnest cussing out was all that Prunes and Matilda would really understand.

As he pushed on along the trail, Lazlo carefully cast back over the brief impressions he'd gotten of his assailants. Nothing in their voices or the dim glimpses he'd caught of them had given him any clue as to their identities. And their heads had been muffled in hoods of some dark material.

Their purpose must have been to rob, which suggested that they knew of his good fortune in the shooting match. If they'd meant to kill, they wouldn't have troubled to mask themselves; they would have used guns or knives rather than clubs. For that reason—even in the violence of the moment—Lazlo had fired after them to scare, not hit, them.

Maybe, he thought grimly, he should have shot with a more lethal intent. He had a lot more at stake than just the winnings of a rifle match.

CHAPTER 5

There were quite a few different ways to hunt for gold. In his lust for riches, Lazlo Kusik had tried all of them. That is, all except the dowsing rod, which some seasoned prospectors swore by—although Lazlo could never understand why. He'd known men who'd spent whole lifetimes tramping the West with dowsing wands fashioned of mistletoe or willow or alder (their preference depending on whatever wood was most available), declaring that "the yellow stuff singing in the earth" would respond to the electricity pouring out of their bodies.

Lazlo's practical mind had scorned that kind of superstitious idiocy out of hand. He'd gone about his own gold-divining with pick and pan and sluice box, and a solid lode of what he liked to think of as good horse sense.

Lazlo had been among the first gold seekers to flock into the Mad Mule River country after word of a gold strike had leaked out and Bozetown, named for the old prospector who had unearthed the first rich pocket of ore, had sprung to slapdash life. Lazlo had staked his own claim at a place far below the camp, where the Mad Mule boiled through a tall arm of rocky hills. Just below that rapids-riddled stretch of river, he had set up his sluice box.

The work had been slow and tedious; it required infinite patience. He had shoveled sandy muck into the long box, opened a floodgate to direct the swift current through the trough, and then scooped out the heaviest gravel by hand so the mud would wash away. He "sluffed" the remaining sand across the backward-pointing wood-baffle fingers and inspected the corrugated metal bottom to ascertain if he'd trapped any gleaming yellow flakes.

Days had dragged into weeks, long and lonely and back-breaking. And above all frustrating. He had endured all kinds of weather and the stinging attacks of insects . . . and the monotonous squeak of the sluice box. Whole weeks had gone by when he hardly turned up a trace of "color." The weeks had slid away into months, and still he had clung to his dogged and driven labors.

Lazlo knew that other placer miners, higher up on the Mad Mule, had found rich scatters of free gold. But the upper river was studded with claims, and his loner instincts had pointed him toward the lower stretches which all reports had declared were far less promising.

Maybe they were. But free gold must move downward, not upward. Lazlo had made his sober gamble, and he was too stubborn to give it up. Maybe it was just a blind hunch. He didn't know.

He had labored all day, every day, under broiling sun or cold rains, running tons of tailings through his sluice box. At day's end he would carefully clean off its baffles and then, stumbling with weariness, would make his way up a hillside to the old deserted trapper's cabin he'd found conveniently close to his claim. He would take the time to prepare a hot and hearty supper, knowing that he must eat well to keep up his strength. Then he would spread his blankets on a heap of fir boughs and collapse into a heavy, dreamless sleep.

It became a sodden and lackluster routine that was tolerable only because Lazlo was too exhausted most of the time to become prey to the boredom and loneliness of it. Once or twice a month, he would take Prunes to Bozetown and load her up with enough grub to last him a few weeks. What little "color" he turned up was spent to supply him with nourishing meals. Boomtown prices being what they were, he just managed to eke out an existence. At that he was often forced to take time out to extend his "boughten" supplies with fresh meat or fish.

Lazlo's ready skill with a rifle ensured that he spent little time on chancy, time-consuming methods of angling for fish which he didn't much care for anyway. Game abounded along

the lower river; the thickets near his cabin were full of rabbit
runways. But experience had taught him that rabbit flesh had
no real nourishment, nothing to give strength to a working
man's thews. So he'd range far afield in a search for elk or
mule deer. If Lazlo were lucky, he would make a quick kill
and have his fill of fresh venison and a good supply for sun-
jerking. The rest of the animal he'd sell to the China Cafe in
Bozetown, and he needed every cent he could get to supple-
ment his meager gold-pickings.

By the time a spring and a summer and most of a fall had
gone by, a leaden discouragement had set in.

Wouldn't it be better just to give up the game and pull out
for other parts? He could always revert to the life of his recent
past—drifting from one job to the next, never working himself
too hard, although he was a willing worker—and he could still
manage to save up a little money between gold-hunting stints.

But that would take time. To Lazlo Kusik, time was the implacable enemy. At thirty-three, he could feel it snapping at his
heels. No, he would not spend twenty more years in the slow
accretion of the wealth he wanted so badly. His goal was the
big, sudden, lavish strike. At least a few men he knew had
"made their score"—why couldn't he? Surely if he persevered,
his time would come. He *knew* it in his bones.

And so it had come. But not by the direct and patient
method that Lazlo had imposed on himself. When he did
locate his strike, it had been by pure chance. At least at the
outset . . .

*   *   *

Lazlo's nerves were pretty keyed-up after the attack as he
was returning from Bozetown to his claim. He sat up most of
that night with a rifle across his knees, keeping out of sight and
trying to stay awake. Yet he dozed off more than once. Then
he would jerk fitfully awake, staring wildly around him . . .

The gray light of predawn was cold and clear. Lazlo was
shivering when, long before sunup, he threw off his blankets
and broke the ice scum on his water bucket. The ice was a
half-inch thick this morning. When he dug a heel at the dirt

floor of his shanty, he found it was frozen ironhard. By noon or so, it would thaw out . . . but that was the strongest sign yet of weather that was rapidly chilling toward winter.

Soon the first snow would come. It might be a light fall; it might as easily be a roaring norther that would close the high passes. Once that happened, Bozetown would be shut off from the outside world—except to those few hardy trekkers who might brave the heights by snowshoe—till late spring. Transporting heavy cargo of any kind across them would be out of the question.

Lazlo wasted no time. After a hasty breakfast, he set to work with rope measure and saw, cutting the oak planks he'd purchased into uniform lengths that would span the bed of his wagon. He sawed the pine two-by-fours into shorter lengths to contrive a system of braces that would support the planks once they were nailed into place.

Before noon, the work was finished. He had outfitted the spring wagon with a false bottom that left a good four inches of space between it and the true bottom. The only exposed side of the shallow compartment was at the back, and that would be concealed once the tailgate was dropped into place. The existence of the compartment would not be revealed by any casual inspection. A slight difference in depth between the outside and inside of the wagon bed was unlikely to be spotted by anyone unless he knew what he was looking for.

Lazlo gathered up the wood trimmings and dropped them in a fire he'd built up. Then he buried every trace of sawdust and stowed his tools out of sight. As he prepared a scanty noon meal over the fire, he considered his next moves. First a coat of paint for the whole wagon, to cover any discrepancy between the seasoned wood and the newly installed planks. Already he had picked over the ore in his hidden cache, separating the pure dust and nuggets from the gold-embedded chunks of dross.

Just the pure stuff added up to a small fortune . . . and the rest could wait in its hiding place till he returned next year. Then, with a crew of helpers he could trust, he would transfer the balance to Saba City. With the considerable amount he

could smuggle across the Elks right now, he'd have till spring
to implement all his plans and make all the necessary arrangements.

Yes. At last he could really dare to believe he was going to
"make it safe to home base." Still the spur of urgency, the
sense of time running out, drove Lazlo on. He wanted to finish
his preparations in a hurry and be ready to roll out by tomorrow.

In the meantime he didn't relax his vigilance.

Hutch Prouter's sly digging had left a deep residue of caution in him. Lazlo had rushed his carpentry work on the wagon
against the possibility that Hutch might pay an unexpected call
at almost any time. However, it hadn't seemed likely he'd
make an appearance before noon. His nightly load of libations
usually kept him dead to the world until noon or later.

A little after midday, Hutch did show up.

By then Lazlo was halfway through his painting of the
wagon; the fresh planks of the false bottom were covered over.
Originally the wagon box had been painted a lead-blue on the
outside, a Venetian red inside, showing that it had been a U.S.
Army vehicle. The new coat, applied by Lazlo inside and out,
was a dull gray.

Hutch didn't seem very interested in Lazlo's activity. He
came tramping heavily into sight along a trail in the bend of
the river. He walked over to Lazlo's fire where, uninvited, he
poured himself a cup of coffee and gulped it down before saying a word. There was a single grunted word of greeting. Lazlo
left off painting one of the Studebaker's sideboards and gave
Hutch a curious glance. Hutch looked in sorrier condition than
could be attributed to a night's carousing. His thick features
had a pasty, sickish cast.

Lazlo put on a look of polite solicitude. "You are feeling a
little off your feed, maybe?" he asked gravely.

"Kind of, yeah." Morosely and without much interest, Hutch
blinked at the half-painted wagon. "What you doing that for?"

"Well, the thing was pretty weathered. I think a new coat of
paint will help to preserve the wood some."

"Uhh." Hutch poured another cup of scalding black brew

and swilled it down. "Jesus, Laz. It is a mighty sorry thing. Almighty sorry."

"What is?"

"About Aussie. I come to tell you he's been murdered."

Carefully Lazlo laid down his paintbrush and then straightened up, twitching a crick out of his back. "What is this? What do you mean? Are you joking with me, Hutch?"

"God, I wish I was. Aussie is stone-dead, little pard, and that's God's truth. He was murdered for sure."

Hutch sat down cross-legged on the ground, running a hand through his matted thatch of hair as he talked. "It happened sometime last night," he said.

This morning Marshal Abe Friendly had noted that Aussie had failed to open his saloon at the usual early hour. That break in routine had seemed odd enough for Friendly to look into it. He had found the padlock on the back door of Aussie's establishment broken and, on the floor just inside, Aussie's cold body. He had been killed by a blow on the head, and the place had been ransacked.

Mechanically, Lazlo bent over and picked up a ragged scrap of cloth. Wiping traces of paint from his hands, he tramped slowly over to Hutch. "Why?" he asked quietly. "Who would kill Aussie? Does Friendly have any idea?"

"Nary a one. I ast him. Whoever done it must o' been looking for something. Money, I hazard." Hutch's big hand paused at the back of his head; he winced. "Jee*zus . . . !*"

"Money," Lazlo echoed. He settled down on his hunkers to face Hutch eye to eye. "I was attacked last night when I left Bozetown. Two men with clubs. I fought them off, but it was a close thing . . ."

"You too?" Hutch's jaw dropped; he stared at Lazlo. "Well, god*damn* now! It happened to me too . . . I reckon the same as to you and poor Aussie."

"You?"

"Damn well told," Hutch said vigorously. "I had took on a good big jag o' tanglefoot and was starting on my way out o' town. I was not steady on my pins and had not got far when—*wham!*—some jasper jumped me. Larruped me over the bean and laid me out cold. When I come to, all the winnings in my jeans, what I hadn't spent buying drinks for half the goddamn town, was plumb gone. Sun was way up by then. Went to tell Abe Friendly what happened. That's when I heerd about Aussie." His eyes narrowed down. "You reckon it were the same crew that give all three of us the what-for?"

"It might have been," Lazlo said in a neutral voice. "You did not see who it was that set on you?"

"Didn't see a goddamn thing. I got larruped from behind, all unawares. How about you?"

Lazlo shook his head. "They had hoods that hid their faces, these men."

"Shitmaroo!" Hutch growled, tenderly rubbing his skull. "Well, they cleaned me out and maybe Aussie . . . 'pending if they found his money. Reckon that's what they was after, what the three o' us collected in bets yestiday."

Lazlo nodded soberly. "It would seem so."

"And that could mean 'most any jaspers in camp who seen the matches or heerd talk about 'em later on." Hutch ran a thick paw through his hair in a final swipe of disgust. "Christ almighty!"

"I am sorry about Aussie. And about your money, Hutch."

Hutch grimaced. "Don't never waste salt o' your tears on t'other fella's grief, little pard. A man has always got enough of his own to sorrow on. If he is up today, you can lay odds he will be flat down tomorrow. That is how the world goes."

Maybe it was just a casual fragment of cynicism. Or was there a deeper meaning hidden in Hutch's words? Lazlo didn't know. But though he had speculations of his own about the attacks on Aussie, Hutch, and himself, he had no intention of voicing them.

Lazlo felt sorry about Aussie but couldn't dredge up any real sympathy for Hutch's loss. He saw no point in mentioning that the weight of his own suspicion fell squarely on the strong, active pair of Colonel Ruddy's performers called "the Altrocchi Brothers." Or that their participation in the assaults— at least in the one on him—would be easy to verify by a knife slash in the one's side, on the other's ankle.

No. All Lazlo Kusik wanted was to get clear of Bozetown, and particularly of Hutch Prouter, as soon as possible. If he'd felt that Hutch deserved better at his hands, it might have been different; he might have done what he could to help Hutch recover his money, even if it delayed his own departure.

The trouble was, he had a pretty fair conviction that Hutch would slit his own brother's throat if he could gain by it. The slight possibility that he might be doing Hutch an injustice didn't cut much ice. In the tough places Lazlo had frequented nearly all his life, a man's survival could hinge on judging the caliber of other men quickly and rightly. And he didn't trust Hutch Prouter. That was all there was to it.

Anyway what had happened to Aussie had left Hutch in a state of mind that was glum and bemused. Consequently he didn't attempt, subtly or clumsily, any more probing into Lazlo's affairs. That was a relief. But there was no telling when Hutch's interest might revive.

Lazlo felt even more relieved when, after a few more blind-alley speculations about the events of last night, Hutch decided to take his leave.

"Just when you figure on packing out o' here, little pard?" he asked.

"Early tomorrow, I think. If this job of painting is dry enough."

"Unh." Hutch scratched his jaw. "Well, you will be coming out along the trail hard by my claim. If t'ain't *too* blame early and I am not sleeping off a load o' corn, I will look for you to drop off for a minute or so, and we will tip a goodbye cup. Hey?"

Lazlo said he would.

They shook hands and Hutch lumbered away. Lazlo watched him till he disappeared around the upriver bend.

CHAPTER 6

Alone now, Lazlo lost no time finishing up the paint job on his wagon. Afterward he tramped up the long ridge above his camp, rifle in one hand, a gunnysack in the other. He crossed the height of land, then went up and down another ridge, keeping a wary lookout all the while.

He hoped that Hutch had really gone back to his claim. It would be easy, once he was out of sight, for him to circle back along the ridges and lay up where he could take a long view of Lazlo's preparations to leave. Still . . . these bald hills had little in the way of good cover, and a watchful man should be able to spot any out-of-the-way movement by a spy.

All the same Lazlo felt nervously exposed as he clambered across the stony crests. His flesh crawled with the thought of what a clear target he might be.

Hutch wasn't his sole cause for worry.

Lazlo couldn't pin down a solid reason for his suspicion of Colonel Laban Ruddy and his crew. Maybe it was the controlled fury he'd noted in Colonel Ruddy's expression after Lazlo had taken the shooting match. Maybe something about last night's hooded attackers had put him in mind of the two wrestlers. Or maybe it was just the cold fact that he and Hutch and Aussie had fetched those "medicine circus" people an unaccustomed upset.

No doubt they weren't used to being outslicked. And Lazlo guessed that probably this was what it really boiled down to. Very likely they had felt driven to recoup their fortunes at the expense of the same three men who were responsible for their heavy losses.

If it had been the "Altrocchi Brothers" who had assaulted

and murdered Aussie last night, they might not have intended to kill him. But Aussie was just as dead. So they might figure they'd have nothing to lose if they should kill again. (If Colonel Ruddy bossed the outfit, if he gave orders to the rest of them—and if he had no large scruples about committing actual murder—wasn't anything possible?)

Having failed in their attempt to rob Lazlo last night, what was to prevent their trying again? Not a damned thing that Lazlo could see.

Outside of Abe Friendly's unofficial regulation of Bozetown, there was no law, no legal retribution of any kind to worry about in this whole wild and wide-open gold-strike country. Every man was expected to shoot his own dogs. The occasional vigilante action against wrongdoers only applied if the offender were caught—and nobody had caught the "medicine circus" people at anything. At anything that could be proved.

Lazlo himself could only admit to a silent suspicion. He wasn't sure of anything. But he couldn't shake a sense of continuing danger. Maybe he was only spooking himself . . . but didn't he have reason to?

Well, the job had to be done. Get it over with fast—that was the main thing.

* * *

Lazlo had discovered the lode by pure accident. Needing meat, he had set out one dawn, working down the river for a half mile in the hope of sighting a deer coming at this hour to drink. He'd found no game but unexpectedly had come on a quantity of shot-size gold nuggets swirling in a rock basin in the river shallows.

Within the hour Lazlo had moved his sluice box there. The place had yielded about an ounce of gold per hour. He noticed something else: The river at this point was half-filled by an alluvial fan of outwash sand and gravel. The hillside above was flanked with rotted, scaling rock from which the debris must have come.

Had the gold also come from up there?

Gripped by a mounting excitement, he had examined the

formation with care, noting that the apex of the alluvial fan, largely obscured by brush, began at the mouth of a deep fissure. Lazlo had clawed his way up the steep incline, avalanches of loose rock cascading away from his driving boots. He had beaten his way through the brush that masked the fissure's mouth and had slogged into the gloom between its towering, crooked walls, still climbing.

Enough light had penetrated into the broad crevice for him to make out the wall of solid quartz that ended the fissure. The band of quartz was maybe six feet in width and just as high. Its surface showed streaks and pits that gleamed a rich yellow in the faint light.

His heart pounding, Lazlo had struck into the rotted granite with his Bowie knife. Big chunks had scaled away with each blow of the heavy blade. After only a half-dozen such blows, he had sunk back on his haunches . . . sweat breaking on his skin, muscles quivering, eyes glazing.

For a moment he'd been almost too stunned to believe what he saw. The broad band of quartz was literally webbed with thick veins of the precious stuff.

He had made it. Lazlo had made his strike.

Almost at once his mind had methodically busied itself with how to make the most of his personal bonanza. First he had applied all the tests for the worthless look-alikes of gold, right out of Bernewitz's *Handbook for Prospectors*. If the stuff couldn't be scratched with a knife, it wasn't pyrite; if it crumbled to powder under the knife, it wasn't pyrrhotite; if it could be beaten into malleable contortions without breaking, it wasn't chalcopyrite. His ore had stood up splendidly to every test.

Grimly, Lazlo had set about keeping his find a total secret. First he'd moved the sluice box back to his claim site and erased the signs of his brief digging in the stream bed below the gold fissure. Then he had continued the daily work on his claim in a lackadaisical way, putting in enough time at it to throw off any casual visitor. One might drop by now and then —Hutch Prouter, who worked a claim a ways upriver, or a few other prospectors. To all of them, Lazlo would complain about his sorry pickings and stress the probability that he'd abandon his claim and clear out of the country before snow-fly.

Each evening after it was full dark, Lazlo would quietly repair a half-mile downriver and spend the night hours in the gold fissure, hewing with his pick and shovel at the band of gold-studded quartz. A big open-sided lantern gave him a strong if shadow-marred light to work by, and its glow was entirely pocketed by the steep walls.

While darkness still held, he would sack up as much of his pickings as he could carry at a time and convey them to a hiding place some distance away. This was a deep rock crevice into which Lazlo would dump the ore and then sift a little sand over the top to conceal it. When dawn's first gray tinged the sky, he would quit work and return to his shack to catch a few hours' sleep before breakfast and another day of idle sluicing.

In spite of his precautions, worry hedged all his waking hours. He'd become as tense as a cat, jumping at every sound, gnawed by a fear that somehow, someone would find him out.

Maybe it was just the suspicious old-country peasant strain in his nature. His Hungarian mother had possessed that quality in full, even though she'd always claimed descent from nobility. His father, a Polish political expatriate, had died shortly after their arrival in America. Lazlo had practically no memory of him.

Just maybe, in any case, he was starting to conjure up threats that didn't exist. Yet he knew that the potential for danger was very real. Ungarnished greed was rampant in any gold camp. The setting attracted that kind of person—and Lazlo recognized himself as one—in swarms. Mix the greed with the lack of ethics in most of the prospectors, add a dash of ruthlessness, season with almost no lawful restraint, and you have constant menace on all sides.

Claim-jumpers were as common as fleas. A man who ran into a good streak of miner's luck might promptly find his claim usurped by another or, as likely as not, by several others. He might be beaten within an inch of his life and thrown off—or even, on occasion, killed on the spot, his body buried in an unmarked grave. The killers would circulate a story that he'd sold out and left the country. Even if anyone could prove otherwise, nobody went to the trouble of collecting the proof. Each prospector had to patrol his own claim, and if he struck anything worthwhile, that could be a day-and-night job.

Lazlo had good reason to take every precaution.

Before the deep pocket of gold-laden quartz was exhausted, he knew he'd made a strike that far exceeded anything that any other prospector had taken out of this region. And he fully intended to take all of it out. Not all in one journey, but if he were to finance the arrangements to get out what remained, he would have to take out a substantial amount now. Therein lay his big problem.

Gold was immensely heavy. Just a block of it, five by five by six inches, weighed nearly a hundred pounds. Lazlo had turned up several hundred pounds of gold-bearing ore, as well as whole nuggets which had fallen free of the rotted quartz. Now that the best of the lode was played out, or seemingly so, he could apply himself wholly to the problem of secretly transporting away as much gold as he would initially require. The assay office in Bozetown itself was equipped to handle far lesser amounts of gold . . . but even if he could have gotten cash for a sizable amount, he was wary about letting anyone in Bozetown, even the camp assayer, know of his find.

Lazlo had toyed with several possibilities, weighing each in turn. Could he transport the gold by stagecoach? Once a week a stage crossed from, and returned to, Saba City on the other side of the Elk Mountains, bringing in or taking out passengers, mail, and cargo of various kinds. That stage run would continue till snow clogged the high passes, and this could happen at any time now. But Lazlo dismissed the notion from his mind anyway. If he loaded even a small part of his fortune on the stage and even a whisper of it leaked out, his treasure would never reach Saba City.

Most likely, neither would he. At least not alive. The stage was a constant target of road agents. Every desperado in the Territory must have held it up at one time or another, in the hope of hitting a good-sized gold shipment.

There was his mule Prunes, but he wouldn't burden her with a load of the size he meant to transport. Lazlo was a man who thought a heap more of animals than he did of most people he'd met, and he was damned if he'd drive a heavy-laden Prunes across the Elks in near-freezing weather. Besides, the danger of being held up and robbed would still be as great.

The answer he had hit on had seemed to him—at the time— a stroke of brilliance. In fact, the idea had excited him so much that he'd decided to act on it at once . . .

* * *

In a rock-littered declivity now, Lazlo sought the deep crevice in which he'd concealed the loads of ore he had conveyed to this spot. He knelt and scraped away some of the sand that camouflaged the cache of pure nuggets. He filled the gunnysack with as much as he could carry.

Staggering under his load, Lazlo started back to his camp— the sack of precious metal slung over one shoulder, his rifle looped over the other with a rawhide thong. Back in camp, he hastily unloaded the nuggets, jamming them into the space between the true and false bottoms of his wagon. He made two more trips back to his cache. The purest part of his treasure was now rammed inside the narrow pockets of the hidden compartment. Any more of it, taken with the weight of himself and his gear, would burden the wagon too heavily. Lazlo dropped the tailgate to cover the open slot at the rear and then nailed it securely into place.

That done, he felt a little queasy from the strain of nerves and physical exertion. By now the sun was fading toward the west. Its thin pale rays held little warmth, but Lazlo was drenched with sweat just the same. He wanted to sit down and rest.

But he had a piece of business to finish up while daylight held. He started to tramp up the ridge again and then was struck by a thought that made him turn back. He got a piece of rope and a small canvas sack out of his possibles. Then he hurried on up the ridge.

Back at the crevice, Lazlo dug into a little hoard of gold

dust that was set off from the chunkier stuff. He filled the canvas sack a third full of the gleaming particles and secured the mouth of it with a drawstring. He tied the sack under his shirt with the rope, patting it out flat against his side so that it made a barely discernible lump.

A hard smile touched his lips. It would not do for a prospector to leave a hard-worked claim with no stake at all under his belt, would it?

Working swiftly now, Lazlo refilled the exposed part of the crevice with sand, then scattered fragments of shale over the seam so it would blend with the rest of this rubble-covered dip. Afterward he headed back for camp, going slowly so he could scan the ground for any telltale signs he might have left. But he'd stuck carefully to bare rock in his comings and goings to his cache. He didn't think that even an Indian could have followed tracks anywhere in the vicinity of the hidden treasure . . .

Just the same, he continued to keep a sharp eye peeled. It was still short of sunset, and the coming of dark wouldn't relieve his anxiety much. He might have waited till nightfall to move the gold, but it would have taken ten times as long, fumbling his way in the dark. And he needed time—not only to let the paint dry on his wagon, but also to rest up for an early morning start out of here.

Tomorrow he would not rest until he had traveled high into the eastern passes, miles from Bozetown and its horde of greedy hardcases.

Lazlo was drag-footed with exhaustion as he tended the mules, gathered wood for a fire, and cooked up a mess of grub. He actually dozed off twice, squatting on his heels while his supper was cooking. It took a vast effort to pull himself alert each time. He wasn't even very hungry, but his body must be fed to keep up his strength. He wolfed down the beans and bacon and pan bread without taste or pleasure. Then he headed for the shanty and some shut-eye.

A sluggish thought hauled Lazlo up short. Maybe he was just light-headed with suspicion, but the idea of spending his last night on his claim in that cramped shack gave him a cornered feeling. Wouldn't it be damned easy for someone to take him by surprise in there?

He got his bedroll from the bunk in the shanty and carried it upslope a ways. Although the crowns of the ridges were bald, there was plenty of brush along their lower flanks. He spread his ground tarp in a hollow place inside a thicket and stretched out. Bundled in his Mackinaw coat and blankets against the increasing chill, his Winchester cradled in his arms, he went quickly to sleep.

A last cold stain of sunlight faded from the sky, but Lazlo was snoring deeply and dreamlessly before it vanished.

* * *

It had been his intention to arise in the first gray light of dawn so he could get as early a start as possible. But Lazlo hadn't reckoned with his own utter weariness.

When he did come awake, suddenly and with a kind of shock, the sun was high in the sky. Christ . . . he must have slept away a good twelve hours or more.

His muscles were stiff with cold as he shed his blankets and got to his feet. God knows, he'd needed the sleep. Too much strain on a man's body and nerves wore him down to a shoestring. That was where he was now, Lazlo knew.

In a few days, he thought, I will be eating prime steaks at the best hotel in Saba City. And washing them down with champagne. It was a promise he had made himself over and over during the most grueling hours since he'd stumbled on his strike.

It was very close to him now. Just a few hours away.

A residue of tension filled Lazlo's belly as he walked down to his camp, but his step was springy, his spirits brisk and almost optimistic. The hour of departure would be later than he'd wished, but he should be packed up and away from here within an hour. Last night he had cooked up enough grub to last him several days. He would make good time on the trail. A few stops to rest the mules and boil up some coffee, maybe a night or two of sleeping out. Then he would be "safe at home base."

Lazlo built his morning fire, added some water and fresh Triple X to the grounds that filled the bottom of his coffeepot, and set the pot close to the fire. Then he carried his few belongings from the shanty to the wagon. The paint job was still a little sticky, but that was all right. A rich man should not mind a few paint stains on his possibles.

The thought made him laugh aloud, suddenly and exultantly.

He sandwiched his prospector's tools among the other gear. All he would leave behind was his sluice box. Maybe some other prospecting fool would try his luck along this stretch of the Mad Mule. He would have need of the sluice box. Lazlo felt cheerful enough to wish that sort of fool well . . .

By the time he had the wagon loaded, the coffee was boiling furiously. Lazlo tramped over to the fire and reached down with a gloved hand to move the pot away from the flames.

A bullet whanged into the coffeepot and set it bounding away.

As the heels of the gunshot crashed against his ears, Lazlo could only stare with stunned disbelief at the perforated pot on its side, the brown liquid gurgling out on the icy ground.

A second shot exploded shards of frozen dirt inches from his boots. It seemed more of a warning shot than anything else. That thought flashed through Lazlo's mind even as he snapped out of his momentary paralysis, turning his head.

He had left his rifle leaning against a rock about twenty feet away. *God!* He should have kept it next to him. His eye gauged the distance, and a clot of reckless anger rose in his throat.

He would make the try. He had to.

Gathering his bunched leg muscles under him, Lazlo made a wild lunge for the rifle. Trying to duck low in the same movement caused him to lose his footing. He felt his feet skid away from under him, and then he crashed on his face.

The unseen rifleman fired again.

This time the flinty chips of earth burst against Lazlo's face. The man had fired that close to it. And he wasn't alone. In the wake of his shot, overlapping it, two other guns spoke at the same time. Both shots gouged up pellets of frozen soil within inches of Lazlo's prone form.

He was trapped. And helpless.

The Winchester was still a yard beyond the tips of his outflung fingers. Lazlo lay very still, feeling the slow trickle of his sweat, the hard pounding of his heart, on the ground beneath him. Slowly, very slowly now, he turned his face toward a growth of brush from which he figured the shots had come.

The foliage rustled. A man stepped out to view. He was stocky and white-haired, with a snapping vigor in his eyes and not a trace of whiskey glaze on them. The rifle in his hands was as steady as a rock; he held it carelessly trained on Lazlo.

"Good morning, Mr. Kusik!"

Ringing out in the crisp young day, Colonel Laban Ruddy's voice was full of hearty good cheer. "Lord alive, lad, but I'm mighty gratified that you decided to show good sense. Who knows? You may still manage to pull out of this unfortunate contretemps with your hide more or less intact . . . eh?"

CHAPTER 7

Colonel Ruddy sat on a boulder and took a long pull at a silver flask he'd taken from the pocket of his belted traveling jacket. The tip of his nose burned with color; a healthy flush of morning chill deepened in his face.

"Ahhh . . . cognac. Nothing but the best. And nothing like it for chasing the cold." Laban tilted a politely questioning brow at Lazlo. "Care for a draught?"

Lazlo shook his head. "No, thank you."

He glanced at the two brothers standing to either side of him with ready pistols. Some Italians, these were. Ruddy had addressed them as "Ab" and "Bije," and had also called one of them "Nephew." He likes to keep it all in the family, Lazlo thought humorlessly. Bije, he had noticed, walked with a slight limp.

"Very well. To business." Laban Ruddy gestured with his flask at the loaded wagon. "I gather, Mr. Kusik, that you're preparing to take your leave of these parts. I should hate to delay your departure. And have no reason to do so if you choose to . . . cooperate?"

"How can I do that?"

"Very easily," Laban said gently. "We want the money you won from us. And others."

"Take it," Lazlo said coldly. "Can I get it out of my pocket?"

"Slowly, if you please. Very."

Lazlo eased the bulging wallet out of his Mackinaw pocket and tossed it at the colonel's feet. Laban Ruddy merely glanced at it and did not pick it up. "So far, so good. Now. The rest, please."

"It is all there. To the penny."

"Not the cash, my dear fellow. Your *gold*. I really feel we have a bonus coming for the inconvenience you've given us."

Laban rose to his feet, took another swig from his flask, capped it, and tucked it away. "Doubtless you've a poke of dust and nuggets to show for your labors. Or you've secured payment for it at the local assay office." His eyes pinched to wintry slits. "We want it. One way or the other, we intend to have it. How will *you* have it, sir?"

Lazlo shrugged. "The pickings were bad. I made enough to buy supplies—that was all."

Laban's big teeth showed below his mustache. "Ha-ha. Is that right. Go through his wagon, Robert. Dump everything out."

The moon-faced Indian—now addressed as Robert Topbear and not as "Wa-nit-ka-we-bo"—was squatting on his heels and looking on with a glum indifference. Now he got up, shambled over to the wagon, and began throwing out its contents. Afterward he tore apart the packs, went over each item piece by piece, and then glanced at Ruddy with a shrug of his brows.

"If he has any gold or any more cash, it must be on him."

"There's a thought," Laban murmured. "Follow it up, why don't you, Robert?"

Robert Topbear patted Lazlo's pockets and the sides of his Mackinaw. His hands paused. He opened the Mackinaw and pulled up Lazlo's shirt. In a moment he'd cut the thong that secured the goldsack against Lazlo's ribs.

Laban gave a weary shake of his head. "You gold grubbers do manifest a singular lack of imagination in concealing your grubbings." He accepted the pouch from Robert Topbear, undid the drawstring, and spilled a portion of gold dust into his palm. He clucked his tongue, regretfully. "*This* is all you've realized from your many months on the spot, Mr. Kusik? I've made, you see, a few judicious inquiries about the length of your sojourn here."

"Men have prospected longer still and have found less." Lazlo laid a bitter tinge of anger on his words. "It is little enough to show for all that time. And now this little is yours, eh?"

"An elementary but accurate conclusion, my dear sir." Laban showed his teeth again as he returned the dust to the bag, cinched it up, and pocketed it. "I believe that concludes our business, and you may resume your preparations for departure . . . which I suggest you undertake without delay. To encourage your swift exodus, we shall appropriate both your rifle and knife. Both of which, by the way, I must congratulate you for wielding so handily."

Lazlo didn't have to simulate the rush of wrath that bit into his reply. "It is too bad Aussie couldn't do the same. Damn your souls!"

"The Australian?" Laban's brows puckered. "True . . . the boys took his purse. But they took your friend Mr. Prouter's, too. So you've heard?"

"Do you tell me you have not?"

"Haven't what? Make it plain, my friend."

"Aussie is dead. You have killed him. Hutch Prouter brought me the news yesterday."

"What?" The word left Laban as a shocked whisper. His gaze, swiveling from one of his nephews to the other, held a mounting fury. "My God! You damned fools! You *killed* a man? After I gave you *distinct* orders to avoid . . . !"

The dull faces of the brothers showed flickers of alarmed bewilderment.

"Jeez, Uncle Labe," Bije got out, "we din't mean to. Christ, we din't even know till now! I hit that funny-talking little jasper, and he folded clean up and we took his money and cleared out. That's all, I vow! We din't know—"

"All right—all right!" Laban cut him off with a chopping motion of one hand. He paced slowly up and down for a moment, staring at the ground, then halted and raised his glare to his nephews. "What's done is done. No way to undo it. But damn your stupid, blundering hides!"

His hard glance cut to Lazlo. "So then. You know. But you can't prove it, can you? Your word against ours. And there are several more of us—to alibi one another. If there were any authorized law to alibi to."

Lazlo said nothing.

"I reiterate, Mr. Kusik: get out. Get clear away from this country. With that word of advice, I bid you good day and wish you well."

"Colonel," Robert Topbear spoke in his flat, dispassionate voice, "I suggest we hold up for just a little while."

"What's that? Why, Robert?"

"This fellow might have a lot more going for him than appearances would indicate." The Indian paused and then nodded at the flint-strewn slope above the camp. "When I was reconnoitering the place a little earlier—before I brought you and the boys word to close in—I came on some diggings way up there. There is a fissure in the cliffs that someone has been digging way back into, I'd say for quite some time. There's a big pile of rubble around the mouth. As though someone"—his black gaze shuttled to Lazlo—"had a good reason for concentrating a great deal of time and effort on the project. And I found this among the rubble."

Robert Topbear produced a rough chunk of rock from his pocket and handed it to Laban. "Those streaks in the rock, Colonel—they might be gold or pyrites. My own guess, it's a piece of gold-bearing ore."

"Really?" Laban squinted at the jagged bit of rock, juggled it in his palm, and looked at Lazlo. "You wouldn't have a plausible explanation for so intriguing a development, would you, Mr. Kusik?"

"I dug up there a long time, sure," Lazlo said stolidly. "That's after I found a little color there. Most of what you got in that sack came out of that same digging."

Laban Ruddy rubbed his goatee thoughtfully. "Mmm. Well . . . the matter bears a bit of study. Robert, I think you might show me the spot. Nephews, just keep your guns on our hunky friend here. See if you can manage not to let him run you both off as you did night before last."

Laban and Robert Topbear went tramping up the slope.

Lazlo sank down on his hunkers by the fire, holding his

hands to the glowing coals, aware of the brothers' watchful gazes and their ready pistols that followed all his movements. Stupid or not, they wouldn't be taken unaware.

Lazlo's thoughts ranged narrowly over his situation. Damn the Indian. If he hadn't spotted the scars of heavy digging, Lazlo would be safely rid of this crew now and not much the poorer for it. How much more could they tell from examining the place? He hoped not much. He had pretty well cleaned out the pocket, and the handful of gold-streaked chips he'd left shouldn't invalidate his story.

He swung to his feet and walked over to the punctured coffeepot.

"Don't you move around like that, Mister," the one called Ab warned him.

"I only wondered if there's a little coffee that didn't spill out."

"You sit," Bije declared flatly.

Lazlo dropped to his haunches and met their dull, unblinking stares with no particular expression.

Presently Laban Ruddy and Topbear returned. Laban was wearing a sleepy, blandly smug look that made a sudden tension coil in Lazlo's belly.

Laban halted before him, a hand thrust in his pocket. "You'd never guess what," he murmured. "Look."

He took the hand from his pocket. In his extended palm lay a solid gold nugget close to the size of a hen's egg. "That's something, eh? Found it under a few inches of dirt I kicked into. Hard to believe you could have missed it, Mr. Kusik. Why, it's again a third of the amount in that poke of yours—I mean, that *was* yours."

Lazlo gave a wondering shake of his head, gazing at the nugget. (It was as large as any he'd dug out of the fissure, and how in God's name *had* he missed it?) "It is quite a thing, for sure. But it might be easy to overlook if it got under some dirt." He shrugged. "It was my bad luck. I have had a lot of that lately."

"You may be in for a bit more." Laban's voice was low, measured, and wicked. "Just possibly you're holding out on us, sir. Could it be you hit a pay streak of considerable value, cleaned it out, and conveyed the cream of it elsewhere?"

"You are imagining things," Lazlo said stonily. "If I did, this smart Indian of yours could track it down, couldn't he?"

Laban smiled thinly. "Robert's talents in the arts of his ancestors are, I regret to say, sadly circumscribed. About the only thing he's ever smelled out with any ultimate conviction is a cache of hooch. If you *did* convey gold in any quantity from that digging, I trust you'd take pains to conceal it from even a trained eye."

Laban sat down on his heels a few yards from Lazlo, folding his arms on his knees. "Come now, Mr. Kusik. Let's not bandy idle words. Your excavation *was* quite productive, wasn't it?"

"That is a guess you can afford. But you guess wrong."

"Do I?" Laban chuckled mildly. "My sense of logic says— quite possibly. But a feeling deep in the gut of me contradicts all logic. Come now, man. We'll have the truth from you by one means or another. How will it be?"

"You have the gold I found. You found it on me. How much does it look like?"

"Offhand," Laban said affably, "I'd say it looks like a blind alley. A decoy. Oh, you're shrewd enough, my boy—in a hunky peasant way. But the trade I've followed lifelong has an old aphorism you may have heard: Never try to con a confidence man."

"I think I heard it a little different."

Laban let out a hearty laugh. "Good. Very good! But now, of course, you'll have to pay the price of such useless intransigence. Boys, relieve Mr. Kusik of his coat. Then march him over to that dead tree yonder and tie him fast to it."

Standing at the north end of Lazlo's claim line, the tree was a small oak, barren of bark, its top broken off, and most of its branches gone. Only the silver-gray trunk endured, rooted in the frozen soil. Ab and Bije used the ropes that had secured Lazlo's pack to tie him upright against the tree, and they made a job of it. His hands were lashed behind him around the trunk. Loops of rope that circled his chest and waist and upper legs also fastened him tightly against it.

Damn his own carelessness!

But drugged with weariness, prodded by haste, working in half-darkness much of the time, it had been easy to lose even a good-sized chunk of gold in the loose earth. No . . . damn the luck that had led Laban Ruddy to uncover the nugget.

Laban gave his orders. He and his nephews and Robert Top-bear would scour the ground all around and above the claim. They were to search every nook and cranny of the surrounding terrain, keeping their eyes open for the least betraying sign.

That, at least, would not do them much good, Lazlo thought with bleak satisfaction. From the original digging, a broken trail of sorts led from the fissure down to his camp: splintered twigs, scuffed ground, bits of broken shale. His many comings and goings had made it inevitable and, bone-tired and ready to drop in his tracks from his other efforts, he'd made no attempt to conceal those signs. But the place where he'd cached the body of his ore was immaculately hidden.

He had one bad moment when Laban Ruddy, poking around the camp proper, laid his gloved hand on the tailgate of Lazlo's wagon. Then he jerked the hand away with a mild curse. The paint was still a little sticky. Would he suspect . . . ?

Apparently not. Laban was too irked by the indelible stain on his fine kidskin glove to attach any importance to the fresh paint job. As Lazlo had told Hutch, it was just a sensible safeguard against weathering. And the damage to his glove diverted Laban from a closer inspection of the wagon.

Somehow that small fiasco of an incident helped Lazlo steel himself against a growing dread. He resolved that, by God, no matter what these bastards did to him, he would give away nothing. *Nothing!*

After nearly an hour of searching, Laban tramped back to where Lazlo was tied. His eyes were red-edged with the heat of impatience and the effects of several more pulls at his flask.

"Here," he said, "is how I have the matter sized. I think you've a considerable cache of gold you've very cleverly hidden somewhere around here. It would be too difficult, for a variety of reasons, to transport it out of the country by yourself just now. But you decided it could afford to wait till a more propitious time. Am I correct?"

Lazlo said tonelessly, "You are the one saying it."

"So far, Mr. Kusik, I have just been playing pat-a-cake." Laban paused. "Be reasonable now. I'll make you a proposition. Show us where the gold is, and we'll divide it straight down the middle. Half for you, half for us. And we'll save you a deal of trouble by conveying it over to Saba City in our three wagons. I'll even return the cash and gold we've taken from you."

"I see." A corner of Lazlo's mouth lifted. "I can see how *you* can call that a fair exchange."

"My dear fellow, nobody said aught about 'fair.' I may just be discussing the price of your survival. Getting a bit chilled, are you?"

Lazlo was. No sun brightened this cold morning. Coatless and immobile, he could feel the chill deepening in his flesh as the minutes crawled on. It was hard not to let his teeth chatter when he spoke.

"I have been colder."

"No doubt." Laban tipped back his head and gazed at the sky. It was a harsh leaden color and clouds boiled over the peaks. "But you'll be a good deal colder yet in a little while, I'll warrant. That sky, now. It could promise rain or sleet or snow." His gaze returned to Lazlo's face. "Why endure needless misery? In the end you'll have to break . . . or perhaps freeze to death."

"There is nothing to tell. Also I do not think you will let me freeze. The killing of Aussie. You did not like that."

"Not at all," Laban said genially. "But I might, with so much at stake, not cavil at letting you freeze a few fingers and toes that would soon require amputation. Think about it awhile."

He turned on his heel and strode away, calling to his nephews and Robert Topbear. When they joined him by the shanty, Laban said, "Boys, our friend over there hasn't decided he'll cooperate. He will, but he needs a space to make up his mind. While we're waiting, we may as well be comfortable. I noticed a stove in the shack. If you fellows will gather some wood, we'll fire it up and be warm in the interim."

The potbelly stove in the shanty was a rusty old affair that Lazlo had used only once; it overheated so badly he'd feared it might burn down the shack. He watched the three younger men round up the needed deadwood from the ridgeside and carry it into the shack. After they'd laid a fire in the stove and had it drawing nicely, the men closed the door of the shack behind them. Smoke bloomed from the roofpipe.

Alone and unobserved now, Lazlo threw all he had into arching his body away from the dead tree, straining against the ropes. It was useless. All he could manage to do was force the knots tighter.

The slate-bellied clouds in the sky were moving overhead now, and the cold was increasing. A raw wind started up. Before long it was picking up a small freight of sleet. Icy rain and pellets of ice slashed against his face and body. The chill was eating into the marrow of his bones now.

Lazlo threw all his strength into another try at escaping his bonds. He knew even as he made the effort how hopeless it was . . .

A tightening of real panic filled his belly.

He had been afraid before now. No man could live for very long as he had, in the places he had lived, and not know what fear was. But this was fear of a different sort. The kind a man knew when he was strapped from taking action against the threat that faced him. He was trussed up like a beast for the slaughter. And he was slowly freezing to death.

Should he give in? Lazlo wavered for a moment.

It would save him from worse. What of Laban Ruddy's promise to share the gold? Half of it would still leave him a rich man. But could he depend on Laban to keep his word? Once he had what he wanted, Laban might even decide to leave Lazlo staked where he was to let the elements finish what Laban had begun.

By now, after all, Laban might have guessed what Lazlo himself damned well knew: that to avenge a steal of this magnitude, he would follow Colonel Laban Ruddy to the ends of hell.

Beyond that was the iron knowledge that he would not knuckle under. Not to any threat under the sun, by God. Part of it was rooted in Lazlo's own stark pride. But weighed into the equation, too, were the endless hours of back-breaking work and nerve-strung worry that had gone into assembling his trove.

It was his. He had earned every grain of it. And he would keep it all, or he would die.

The door of the shack opened. Robert Topbear came out, stumbling a little, toting a wooden bucket that Lazlo had left in the shack. He carried it down to the stream bank and filled it with water. Unsteadily he crossed the open space to Lazlo, the full bucket sloshing at his side.

Laban Ruddy had been watching from the open door of the shack. Now he let out a loud, immoderate laugh and went back in, closing the door.

Robert Topbear halted and gave Lazlo a lopsided leer. "Paleface decide talk now? Uh? Tellum red brother where yellow wampum hid? Uh?"

"All the moonshine is not in your head." Lazlo's lips were stiff, his teeth chattering fiercely now. "There is no gold. Go back, damn you, and tell your master that."

Robert Topbear seemed to take no offense. Still grinning, he glanced down at the bucket he held. "The colonel thought you might still feel just so. That's why he sent me to fetch a pail of water to throw on you. Get a little colder than you are, you might make up your mind faster."

"Go ahead then. Don't keep your master waiting."

For answer, Robert Topbear tilted the bucket in his hands and poured all the water out on the ground. Even in his frozen, half-torpid misery, Lazlo felt a feeble dart of surprise.

"Why?" he murmured.

Robert Topbear's grin faded. "Maybe because liquor never makes a dirty job taste any better."

"This bothers you? You're the one told him maybe I had more gold hid somewhere."

Topbear grimaced. "I didn't think about what it might lead to. The colonel—" He paused and rubbed a hand over his face, as if scraping away the effects of drink he'd consumed. "The colonel wasn't always like this. Always a con man, sure, and a sharper. But he's never been an out-and-out thief before. Nor a man who'd do to another what he's doing to you. Christ, I don't know. Maybe all the booze he takes has eaten into his brain."

Lazlo set his jaws to keep his teeth from rattling together. He spoke through his nearly clenched teeth. "It's good it has not eaten into yours."

"Oh, I don't know." Robert Topbear gave a wry, bitter shrug of one shoulder, as though the irony were lost on him. "I have no morality, you know. Not the integrity of my own people anymore. Not even the morality of you whites, which amounts to damned little. Had a good moral sense once, years ago before I was packed off to the White Father's Indian School at Carlisle, Pennsylvania."

"Is that where you got to reading Cooper?"

Robert Topbear's grin flashed and vanished. "Spotted that, did you—in my spiel? You're sort of a surprising fellow on your own account. Yes, Cooper. And a lot of other things. Learned a hell of a lot about the white man's vastly superior culture. Enough to graduate at the head of my class at Carlisle. Then went back to my reservation in the Nations. But I no longer fitted into the tribal life. Had learned too much, you see. And soon found I did not fit into the white man's society any better. You paragons of the master race don't much fancy uppity Injuns. Especially eddicated-up-to-their-ears ones."

Topbear smiled crookedly; he made an aimless gesture with the empty bucket. "Ah well. Mine's no special case. Happens to a lot of us. When the booze gets working, I talk too damned much. My apologies."

"That's why you got drinking?"

Lazlo said the words with no censure and no real interest. He was too miserable to give a damn. Hurtful needles of cold were tingling into his fingers and toes, driving with a quiet agony into the ends of all his nerves.

"That's why. And why, I guess to my good fortune, I fell in with Colonel Ruddy. He's been more than my employer. He has been"—Topbear hesitated—"my good friend."

"What does he pay you in? Booze?"

A gleam of anger surfaced in the Indian's black eyes. Then he relaxed; his crooked smile flickered again. "What else? But he's been kindly to me. He has kept me with him when, at times, he might have found it convenient to abandon me. Worth a drop of loyalty—don't you think?"

"What I think," Lazlo said coldly, "is that the brains of you both, you and Ruddy, are rotted with whiskey. I would not think that two of you could get so much out of one flask."

Robert Topbear chuckled. "You underestimate the resources of a dedicated boozer, friend. Both the colonel and I have—or had—a few other flasks secreted about our persons."

"I am not surprised. Does the shootist drink too?"

"The what?"

"The lady with the special Henry rifle. She seems to take up with a man's ways pretty good."

"Oh, Stella. She's the colonel's daughter. Older one, I mean. The Princess Shahazar is the other one. Her real name is Myra Mae. 'Member the princess?" Robert Topbear made a few roguish gyrating motions with one hand. "Nope, Stell is a real decent woman."

"It seems so. Otherwise why would she help you sharp the suckers?"

Robert Topbear's glint of humor switched off.

"Watch what you say about her," he said flatly. "Stella Ruddy is a good woman. Sure she talks rough and dresses like a man, mostly to spite her pa. But she has no part of his con act—or mine." Topbear's speech was starting to slur as the full intake of the liquor he'd consumed hit his brain; he blinked rapidly as if to focus his eyes. "Fact is, what the colonel tol' the girls this morning was that he and I and the two boys were going to town for an all-day whoop-up. Meaning, natch'ly, we meant to get falling-down drunk."

"They would have no trouble believing that."

"Natch'ly not."

"In a minute," Lazlo gibed, "I think you will fall on your face anyway. And how will you tell your master why you did not wet me down? I think that will make him mad."

Robert Topbear gave a loud, hiccoughing laugh. "Who'n hell gotta wet you down, f' krissake? You're damn near soaked through already, paleface. Give you another fifteen minutes out here, you be too damn stiff to sing out, even if you decide to talk. Huh?"

Lazlo didn't reply.

Robert Topbear swayed on his braced legs, laughed again, and then turned and lurched back to the shack.

Icy shudders wracked Lazlo's body. He was wet to the skin, all right, and he could feel the last tinglings of sensation ebbing out of his extremities. They were going totally numb.

Maybe you should give in, he thought. What good is gold to a dead man? Maybe they will take it all, but a dead man could not even care.

Panic was edging out resolution now, and he fought the temptation with all his will. Once more he heaved savagely against the pinioning ropes. They held tight.

But he felt a faint grating at the base of the tree. What was that? Wasn't it set as solidly in the frozen earth as it appeared to be?

Again Lazlo threw his weight forward and then back, rocking against the trunk. There was a sharp crack. From the main root of the dead tree? He kept on steadily and fiercely rocking, a burst of hope feeding fire into his sluggish blood.

Suddenly the tree was grinding loosely in its moorings. Then the last of its network of dead roots gave way and pulled free.

Tipping suddenly forward, Lazlo fought for balance and barely gained it before he fell on his face. God, that must not happen.

For a moment he stood half-bent under the tree's dead weight, mustering the dregs of his energy. His feet, now that he could move again, felt like frozen blocks. He must be very careful. Now he could move a little, even walk a little, but he must go very slow and careful. If he fell down, trussed up as he was, he would never be able to get back on his feet.

At any moment one of the men in the shack might come out again. So he had to get away from here. That came first. Then he must find help.

Hutch. Hutch Prouter's claim was the nearest place. A little distance up the Mad Mule on this side of it. If he could get to it before his half-escape was discovered . . .

Reeling awkwardly toward the north edge of his claim, Lazlo set a painfully turtlelike pace, taking every step as gingerly as a girl with her legs encased in a hobbling skirt. Some of the freezing sleet had crusted on his clothing; it sloughed away in crackling scales as he inched along. He had to keep bent way over just to keep the lower part of the tree trunk on his back from hitting his heels. He staggered and stumbled. He took each step a few inches at a time and with infinite care.

He couldn't even feel his feet any longer. Their clumsy wooden strides at the ends of his stiffened legs, the numbing cold working steadily upward, made him wonder if the rest of him would also give out before he got much farther.

At the same time he felt a driving and dogged urge not to waste a precious second. Now he was away from the open bank on the upriver trail, deep in the trees and out of sight of the shack. Raging against his own near helplessness, he pushed himself too hard. His boot skidded in a puddle of icy slush.

Lazlo twisted as he fell, but all he saved himself from was landing on his face. He landed on his side instead, and he was just as helpless.

He made one mighty effort to tuck his feet under him, to maneuver himself upright, and knew even as he made the try how hopeless it was. He sank back. A groan of despair burned in his chest; the sweat of his rage and his futile efforts began to ice on his face.

He heard a clump of booted steps on the frozen trail. They were coming after him—*damn them to hell!*

The boots came into the tail of his vision. They stopped less than a yard from his head. With his residue of failing strength,

Lazlo craned his head enough to let his gaze travel up along the muffled, burly form of the man who stood above him.

"Howdy there, little pard," said Hutch Prouter. "You been caught in a mite of a jackpot, now ain't you?"

CHAPTER 8

Hutch cut him free and dragged him deeper into the trees. Then Hutch shucked off the heavy buffalo-hide coat he was wearing and wrapped it around Lazlo. Even in this weather it had a thick, musky, unpleasant smell, but Lazlo couldn't remember a more welcome warmth. He crouched on the ground with his back to a tree, huddling inside the coat as Hutch briefly told him how he'd come to be here.

Earlier, from his own tree-hidden camp by the river, he had seen Colonel Laban Ruddy and his companions coming along the trail, headed downstream. What were they doing way out here, and where were they going? The question had piqued Hutch enough for him to follow them, keeping out of sight.

Watching from the edge of timber, he'd seen all that had occurred between Lazlo and the colonel. But he couldn't overhear their words and wasn't quite sure what to make of the situation. Being unarmed, he'd decided that if he were to be of any help to his "little pard," he'd better go back to camp and fetch his guns. Having done so, he returned to the spot just as Lazlo had taken his helpless spill.

Hutch was eyeing him closely, brows raised as he talked.

Lazlo answered the unspoken question. "They came to rob me like they did you and Aussie. Yes, it was them did that. Then . . . they thought I had more gold than I do. So they made me freeze awhile so I would talk."

"And you wasn't about to, huh?"

"There was nothing to tell."

Hutch nodded and scratched his beard. "Unh. Well, you are out of one jackpot of trouble, little pard. What now?"

Lazlo's teeth were chattering with cold, but some feeling had flooded back into his chilled body. He could move his arms and legs without much trouble. Sensation was trickling back into his fingers and toes. He flexed them to help the feeling along, ignoring the prickles of pain.

"You went and got your guns," he murmured. "Good. That is how things stand now."

Hutch hefted his old Hawken rifle in one fist. His Walker Colt was rammed into the waistband of his leather pants. "Surest thing you know. You want to roust them gents around some, I take it."

"Yes," Lazlo said gently. "Some."

A silent chuckle shook Hutch's vast bulk. "I got a score to settle with 'em too, Laz. You just say on. I reckon we can light a hotter fire under their britches than they got going in yonder shack."

There were two ways they could come at the shack's occupants: by the door or by a small window over on the south wall. Lazlo figured that he and Hutch could catch the four men between them, and by complete surprise, if they worked in unison.

Hutch nodded. "You want to hang up their hides for good? The Lord hisself couldn't blame you none."

"No. Take them alive if we can." But Lazlo's jaw had an iron set. "Only shoot if we need to."

On stiff legs he moved back to the edge of timber and paused, sweeping a glance over the cabin and the clearing. Ruddy or one of the others might come out at any moment to check on him. But that wasn't what claimed Lazlo's immediate attention. His rifle was still leaning against the same rock. Once they'd had Lazlo in hand, Ruddy and his men had carelessly left it there.

He wanted his own rifle, the good familiar feel of it in his hands. Let Hutch keep both his antique weapons.

Hulking beside him, Hutch said impatiently, "All right now, Laz. We going ahead or not?"

Lazlo said, "Yes," and added a few terse details as to what he had in mind. Then they broke apart, Hutch lumbering toward the door like a great stalking bear, while Lazlo cut across to the rock. His circulation was coming back; his movements were smooth and quick as he picked up his rifle and checked the action.

Another short run and he was over by the south window.

Glass windows weren't a feature of any building in or around Bozetown. Glass was an expensive indulgence to have freighted in, and it broke too easily. What you did, if you furnished your shelter with any sort of window, was to outfit it with a scraped deerhide that was translucent enough to let in light. Or else you covered the aperture with a pegged-together square of puncheon boards that swung inward on rawhide hinges fastened to a side of the frame.

The window of Lazlo's shack was covered with a puncheon-board square. Weathering and warping had strained the puncheons apart, leaving broad cracks through which a man could scan the whole interior.

Three of them—Colonel Ruddy, Robert Topbear, and Bije —were sitting on their heels in a circle, intent on what appeared to be a game of poker, casting the greasy, well-thumbed cards down on the packed-clay floor. Both Topbear and the colonel looked as if they might slide over on their faces at any moment. Gaps in the old stove sent out a fitful orange glare over the scene. The one called Ab was crouched by the stove, not too steady himself as he fed a few lengths of stovewood into the fire.

Carefully, rifle balanced in his left hand, Lazlo planted his right hand against the puncheon square. Suddenly he swung it in, slapping his right hand to the barrel of the rifle and thrusting his arms and head and shoulders through.

He fired into the ceiling.

The shot was thunderous in the shack. It was the signal to Hutch, who gave the door a mighty kick that burst it open. He came barreling into the room. His face wore a huge grin; his Walker Colt was leveled.

The three men on the floor froze in place. Ab came wheeling about wildly, dropping the stove pieces. Then he clawed at the pistol thrust in his belt.

"Don't!" Lazlo yelled, bringing the rifle to bear.

He was pumping its lever on-cock even as Ab yanked his gun free. And Lazlo fired.

The slug's force flung Ab against the wall with an impact that shook the building. He slid down to a sitting position, his eyes already glazing. They turned a last puzzled, unfocused look on his uncle; his mouth opened and worked, as if laboring for speech.

No words came. His head tipped over on his shoulder. The sudden pungence of his released sphincter filled the hot closeness of the room.

A fan of cards in Colonel Ruddy's upraised hand dribbled to the floor. "Ab, boy?" he whispered. "Ab, boy?"

He scrambled on his hands and knees to his nephew's side. His hand searched for a heartbeat. When he pulled the hand back, his palm was a slick wet red and he stared at it, unbelieving.

"On your feet," Lazlo ordered. "Up. Up, damn you! Hutch —their guns, their knives—"

Robert Topbear obeyed, looking sober and careful. Ruddy stayed as he was. So did Bije, his swarthy face shocked and almost uncomprehending. Hutch moved among them, collecting pistols and knives. These he tossed into a corner alongside the rifles leaning there.

"That does it, Laz."

"Keep a watch on them."

Lazlo withdrew from the window and tramped around to the door. He ordered the men outside. Robert Topbear didn't have to be told twice. But Lazlo had to repeat the order three times to get the grief-stunned Bije and the colonel in motion.

They stood in the cutting, sleet-freighted wind that couldn't quench the burn of hatred in the faces of Ab's kinsmen. Both of them still managed to stare straight at Lazlo, grief already submerging itself in a wish to do hot-blooded murder.

Tears iced on Bije's cheeks. "Mister," he said in a quivering voice, "you gonna kill us too, you better do it quick and do it now. I swear, you hold off and I will kill you." His powerful hands flexed and unflexed. "I will do it with no weapons a-tall."

"I was you, Laz," Hutch said mildly, "I would take this boy at his word."

"Shut up, Hutch." A hard pulse pounded in Lazlo's head. "I did not ask you."

"You hear me all the same. Now this sharper and his crew, by God, they killed Aussie and robbed me and set you out to freeze. If that ain't cause enough to put 'em under, they will hang your hide up for sure any chance they get. Look at that old sharper, now. Look at his face."

The colonel's skin had a yellowish pallor and hugged the lines of his skull as if he'd aged many years in a few moments. "Your friend has the right of it, Mr. Kusik," he said. "Perhaps you should heed his word."

"But it will work two ways," Lazlo said quietly. "You will kill me on sight if you can. But I will do the same . . . next time. That is a fair warning. I am very good with a rifle—this you know. So maybe you better see there is not a next time."

"Ah, but there will be." Rimmed by a drip of frosty whiteness that tugged down its ends, the colonel's mustache made his meaningless grin even more grotesque. "And you will not seek us out, I think. But *we'll* be looking for you, sir. Enjoy any speculations you may have on exactly who will have the advantage . . ."

While Hutch held a gun on them, Lazlo thoroughly searched the three prisoners. He recovered his own gold pouch and money from Laban Ruddy and turned up a bulging money belt cinched around Laban's waist. It contained a good deal of both coin and paper money. In the pockets of Robert Topbear and Bije Willet and the dead Ab, he found only a few loose bills and coins. Altogether, it came to somewhat more than what he and Hutch and Aussie had divvied up between them.

Hutch vigorously declared that they'd be justified in appropriating all of it. But Lazlo scrupulously counted out to the cent what Laban's nephews had taken from them. He didn't know how Laban and his cohorts had come by the rest of it and did not care. He stuffed the remaining money in the money belt and handed it back to Laban.

"And now," Laban said with a wintry smile, "you think that evens our score, hunky? Not by my lights it doesn't."

"I did not think it would." Wearily Lazlo motioned at the upstream trail. "All of you clear out. Do not bother coming back for your guns. They will be at the bottom of the river."

He and Hutch watched them tramp away into the woods, Bije bearing his brother's dead weight across his shoulders. Hutch shook his head, grumbling, "Boy, you're making one pluperfect awful mistake. Couple of 'em, I'd say."

"I am not a killer. And a man does not stay honest by robbing even a thief. So far, Hutch, I have stayed honest."

"But Jesus—!"

"Why don't you chuck their guns and frogstickers in the river? Then we'll cook up something to eat, eh?"

To that, anyway, Hutch had no objection. While he disposed of the weapons, Lazlo went into the shack and stripped down and toweled himself dry in the stove's heat; then he put on dry clothes. Afterward he tended his mules and whipped up a sizable batch of beans and bacon and sourdough biscuits, of which he and Hutch hungrily woifed down about a third. The rest of it Lazlo packed up for the journey ahead. Once on the trail, he intended to make as few halts as possible; he would eat while on the move.

It was too late, now, to cover much distance in what remained of this day, and Lazlo was dog-tired from his latest ordeal. It would be best if he caught at least a few hours' sleep before starting out.

Hutch, slumped at ease in a rawhide-rigged chair—the cabin's only piece of furniture besides a pole bunk built into one wall—belched and picked his teeth reflectively. "Y' know, Laz," he said idly, "I been thinking. Maybe what I ought to do . . . I ought to ride out o' these mountains with you. Give you an escort, sort of. That ole medicine drummer and his boys will be looking to deadfall you som'eres up ahead. I lay you any odds on it."

Lazlo was sitting on his haunches by the stove. For answer, he reached in his coat pocket and scooped out the money he'd recovered, spilling it out on the clay floor. He divided it into two separate and equal piles and pointed at one. "That is yours, Hutch. To the penny. In it is half of Aussie's share. I think this squares us, and now we go our ways, eh?"

Hutch looked injured. "Why, little pard, I allowed you would be grateful for the offer."

"I am. But I do not like to owe a man, and already I owe you too much. Also, if there are dogs to be shot, I will shoot my own. That is how I do things. Thank you."

Hutch grumbled, but he'd learned to know the steely under-core that sometimes touched Lazlo's voice and what it meant. No argument.

Once more Lazlo wondered silently if he'd possibly mis-judged Hutch. And still concluded he hadn't. Hutch's appear-ance just when he'd needed help had been almost too timely. Mightn't Hutch have been prowling around the camp on his own, looking to spy on Lazlo's activities, just before Laban and his people had shown up?

Well, Hutch declared in a morosely aggrieved voice, if that's how his little pard wanted it, he'd say no more. But he still hoped Laz would drop by his camp for a cup of coffee right after he pulled out.

Lazlo politely said he would. And Hutch took his departure.

Edged by his suspicions, Lazlo curled up in the brush near the shack, bundled in blankets and with rifle at hand. The fall of sleet was letting up, and its few light cold pings on his face couldn't prevent him from dropping into a sound sleep . . .

CHAPTER 9

When he awoke, the last traces of daylight were washing out of the sky. Soon it would be fully dark. Feeling sharply refreshed, he made his final preparations to leave and hitched Prunes and Matilda to the wagon.

At the same time his mind ranged bleakly over what might be ahead of him. Three men would be "laying for" him, and the advantage would rest with them. They might get hold of more guns and try sneaking up on his camp again. But more likely they would bide their time. Lazlo would be burdened with a slow-moving wagon and the need for keeping his full attention on the rough crossing of the Elks. At least twice on the way he'd be compelled to slack his guard in order to catch a little sleep. Once they had him spotted, Ruddy and company could either overtake him or ambush him . . . quickly and by surprise.

Then Lazlo paused on a thought: *But they will look for me on the road to Saba City. There is another way . . . and being so new here, they will not know of it.*

Another way, yes. But it was across a brutally rugged stretch he'd never think of tackling otherwise. Trevo Pass, cutting through the first western ramparts of the Elks, led to a maze of trails that could be crossed on foot by a man who knew them. Lazlo had done it himself twice. But could a heavily loaded wagon get across?

Head bowed, his hands resting on the harness, Lazlo weighed the idea with care. Carson's Crossing lay on the far side of that mountain arm, and it had an assay office. But it was even farther away than Saba City. What if his wagon broke down on a remote trail? Against those natural perils, however, he balanced the dangers posed by Ruddy and company, as well as by assorted road agents, along the well-graded way to Saba City.

Do you really mind a good gamble so much, my practical fellow? Then maybe you are in the wrong business.

With the wry flicker of a grin, Lazlo swung to the wagon seat and took up the reins, hoorawing the mules into motion. For a moment they strained against the wagon's weight. Then the vehicle stirred and rolled forward, and he knew it would be all right. At least on the early part of the trail . . .

A light sleet continued to prickle his face as he pushed through the gathering dark. Ahead was Hutch's camp, and he'd already made up his mind not to stop if he saw no fire. Hutch *did* know this country, and if he got an inkling of what Lazlo was up to, it would be dangerous knowledge.

Slowly, almost noiselessly, Lazlo eased his team along the road where it curved past the dark grove that hid Hutch's camp. Any glimmers of firelight would show among the trees. But he saw nothing. Hutch had to be asleep, and his fire, if he'd laid one, had died to ashes. Yet Lazlo winced every time his wheels banged against bumps in the frozen trail.

Trevo Pass was very close now, and there was enough light to show where it breached the looming bluffs. He swung slowly into it and gave the mules their head along a narrow trail that ran through rank brush on the canyon floor. The wheels jolted across the rocky roughness, and the wagon sent out a few creaks of complaint but not many. He drove steadily and carefully along the bottom of the pass for about an hour. The sharp thrust of bluffs that marked the first rise of mountains to the west dwindled into a long wedge of flatlands. The trail took a winding course across these flats, beyond which the tough part of his journey would begin.

Then the snow began to fall.

It came down lightly at first, a swirling handful of flakes that mingled with the pelting sleet. Quite suddenly the rattle of sleet on the wagon box ceased, and there was only the spatter of wet snow, thickening fast.

Lazlo hadn't counted on anything like this. He damned his

luck with a heartfelt anger. There was always a possibility of early snow in the high country this late in the year, but it had seemed a minimal risk. There'd seemed little danger that in the few days it would take to cross the peaks, the fates would conspire to dump a fall of snow on his trail. Now it was happening.

Lazlo pulled up the team, considering. He could turn back. And what then? Be stalled in the Bozetown diggings for a winter? With Ruddy and his comrades maybe hanging about too, waiting their chance? And what of Hutch Prouter?

His anger prodded up stubbornness. He would go ahead. The risk of getting bogged down in mountain snows seemed less chancy than what lay behind. These early-season snows were only harbingers; almost always they melted off in a day or so.

He urged the team into the whirling whiteness, unable to make out anything beyond a few yards away, not even the mules' heads.

Then, out of the white-black silence, Lazlo heard a muffled tramp of feet. Someone was coming along the trail behind him. He hauled up the team and picked up his Winchester, now kept always ready to hand. He strained his eyes against the pale-shot darkness.

Gradually a man's form came hulking into sight. By his size, Lazlo knew at once who it was. But the knowledge only sharpened his wariness.

"Hutch?"

"Surest thing you know, little pard," came the cheery reply. "Yes sirree . . ."

Hutch halted by the wagon, a bulging warbag slung across one shoulder, and rested a great paw on the sideboard as he squinted up at Lazlo. "Didn't see no sense to hanging on at Bozetown this winter. Have had mighty poor diggings in them parts. That being so, I figured I would pack up and 'winter-warm' over in Saba City or Carson's Crossing, either one."

"I see." Lazlo managed to keep his voice even. "So then, can I ask what makes you decide to do so right now?"

"Oh, I got thinking on't a goodly spell back," Hutch said

amiably. "But I didn't really get to considering it till I knowed you was fixing to pull out. I taken a powerful shine to you, little pard. I figured if you did not mind, it'd suit me to share your fortunes for a time."

"Is that right."

"Surest thing, you know. I mean, hell, what you objected to afore is me siding with you in any more rows with that colonel and his crowd. Shit, Laz, I understand how that be. Man is got his pride. But ain't no reason I couldn't give you a mite o' company so far as Carson's Crossing, was there now?"

"That is something else." Lazlo peered through the beating snow at the outline of Hutch's shaggy head. "How did you know I went this way?"

"Didn't take no broad-gauge guessing, boy. I was rolled up for the night when I heard your wagon go by my camp. I'm a light sleeper and got ears like razors; they are that sharp. Then I heard your wagon turn into Trevo Pass. Sound carries from atwixt them stone walls to beat all hell. So I thought, shit, that makes sense. It come to ole Laz it is the safest way he can clear out. Me, I was fixing to pack out anyway (would of told you as much if you'd dropped by), and so might's well side you out right away. War'n't no great doing. Cached what good-sized odds 'n' ends I own, tools 'n' such, out o' sight for when I return, come spring. Chucked them few light possibles I possess in my warbag, and I was all geared up. Then took me a little deal o' walking to catch up—that's all."

"Convenient," Lazlo murmured. "Very. But it is a tough trip over these peaks."

"Well, that's another thing. Figured you would be pleased to have an assist along the way. Laz, there is places ahead that you will be obliged to practic'ly lift them goddamn mules and wagon acrost. You be glad of an exter pair of strong arms 'bout then. 'Sides, I know the trails 'long this way good as you do. Anything at all should happen to you—an accident like— be me to pull you through. Sort of life insurance, huh?"

Lazlo couldn't make out but could easily picture the broadly cheerful grin that must be shaping Hutch's lips. Yet what he'd said was true. For the moment Lazlo could think of no ready argument to counter the glib offer. Still, whether Hutch was sure of anything or not, he must be downwind of the truth.

Damn him! But what do I do? If I refuse now, he will be sure. But what is to prevent him from following me and waiting . . . till I am dead for sleep? Wouldn't it be better to keep Hutch squarely under his eye? The frying pan could not be any hotter than the fire.

"Done, Hutch!" Lazlo reached down and gave the bigger man a friendly slap on the shoulder. "You will be a welcome companion. You surprised me is all, coming upon me so sudden."

"Yeah." Hutch might have been a little disconcerted. If so, he covered it by adding, " 'Course I was a mite peeved, you not stopping by my outfit like you promised."

"Your fire was out," Lazlo said with a forced joviality. "When Hutch Prouter is full of booze, he is dead to the world as a man can be, eh? I would not disturb your sleep."

"Oh, yeah. Well, I didn't drink nothing stronger'n river water last night."

"Why, now I see it is so." Lazlo shifted sideways on the seat. "Come up beside me and ride. Throw your pack in the wagon."

Hutch laid his warbag in the wagon bed with lighthanded care, explained by a distinct clink of bottles. *Maybe,* Lazlo thought grimly, *he looks to booze to give him belly for a nasty piece of work . . . but how can I be sure?*

He couldn't be. Otherwise he'd do what he must to protect his gold and his life. But Lazlo's conscience chained him to certainties where right and wrong were concerned. He *had* to be sure. So he would have to wait. And stay alert. Somehow he must manage to do both, during this long crossing of the mountains. Even if it lasted only a few days, it would still be the longest trip of his life.

And maybe the last.

* * *

Soon the falling snow slacked off to a few drifting flakes. At least the way ahead would not be blocked by deep snow. Unless another storm came along soon, and that wasn't likely.

Hours passed. The double strain of guiding the team along a mushy nightbound trail and worrying about the man beside him told badly on Lazlo's nerves. Before long he would need rest and sleep. How could he get them?

The wagon creaked more than ever as it jolted along the rough road; Hutch's vast weight caused the whole vehicle to lean increasingly askew on that side. Lazlo was about to say so when Hutch himself spoke up affably: "Seems I am adding a passel exter to the load. Mought be best I light down and mosey 'long on foot."

Lazlo stopped long enough for Hutch to clamber down and then shook the mules into motion again. By now his visibility was better. He could make out details of the wide flats they were crossing: trees, boulders, even the black humps of distant bluffs against a lesser darkness of sky. The only sound was a crunch of hoofs and wheels on crisp new snow.

Hutch's heavy tread should also have been loud in the snow, but Lazlo suddenly noticed that it wasn't. A quick glance showed him that Hutch was no longer tramping beside the wagon. He'd fallen back behind it, striding along with head bent, as though scanning the ground.

Lazlo no longer needed to guess. He knew.

A moment later Hutch was back trudging alongside the wagon. What he'd been studying, of course, were the deep-sunk ruts of the wagon's wheels in fresh snow. The wagon was a light one; if it were heavily weighted in any way, the wheelprints would show as much. Not that a cursory examination of the ruts would leave Hutch really sure of anything. What mattered was that he'd given himself away. Lazlo could be sure now that Hutch posed a certain and murderous danger to him.

Soon he must somehow make a move before Hutch made one. But God—what move? Would he be forced to kill the man in cold blood?

Maybe not. Lazlo felt a sudden leap of hope.

Staring ahead of the team into a slowly lightening darkness as false dawn drew on, he saw the faint prints of wagon wheels in the snow. Another party had put a wagon, in fact several wagons, into the westward pass ahead of him. They'd come this way just hours before, the night's snowfall having only partly obliterated their wheeltracks at this point. They weren't very far ahead.

Hutch also saw the ruts and dourly commented on them, grumbling, "Blamed funny thing, any folks choosing a way acrost these peaks this time o' year."

"Yes," Lazlo agreed soberly. "It is strange, all right."

Pretty soon the tracks were more clearly defined, showing how far the wagons had gotten when the snow had ceased falling. He would, Lazlo knew exultantly, overtake them before long.

Meantime he kept a close watch on Hutch.

CHAPTER 10

Within another hour, as the dawn light grew, the white land-scape ahead was broken by a motte of pines. The trail led into it. Through the trunks now, Lazlo made out ruddy gleams of firelight. The sound of childish voices and laughter drifted toward him.

So many kids, he thought, must mean a large party. But he was baffled. What kind of people (discounting his own case) would be fool enough to try crossing the high passes at this time of year—with wagons and children?

Before Lazlo and Hutch reached the camp, a young man came tramping out of the woods to their right. He was bearing an armload of dead branches.

"Hello," he said pleasantly.

Lazlo pulled to a full stop, gave him a civil nod, and then glanced at the young girl, who was also carrying a load of branches, and had now moved up beside the man. She was small and dark, quite pretty, and he guessed not over fourteen. She had a fresh, scrubbed look that was nice to see, and her shy, quiet manner did it justice.

"I'm Mark Bly, and this is Cissie O'Halloran," said the young man. "We were out gathering wood when we heard your wagon coming."

"That is your camp ahead?"

"It is. If you gentlemen would care to breakfast with us, you'd be welcome."

Mark was tall and gangling, probably not much past twenty. He had a courteous and well-spoken way about him. His thatch of crisp carroty hair topped an open, trusting face that Lazlo immediately liked.

Glancing at Hutch, Lazlo said, "That sounds fine, eh?"

But Hutch paid no attention. He was gazing at Cissie O'Halloran with a kind of lewd, slack-jawed grin. The girl saw it too. She moved a little closer to Mark and lowered her eyes. Lazlo had never seen this side of Hutch, and it wasn't reassuring to note.

Lazlo felt a mounting curiosity as he put the wagon into the grove, following Mark and Cissie into a wide natural clearing. Three covered wagons were drawn up in the trampled snow to one side; their team mules were hobbled nearby. There were kids all over the place, chattering and yelling and clowning around . . . both boys and girls. But no sign of adults that he could see. *What sort of outfit is this?* he thought in bewilderment.

The kids were working mostly in twos, coming out of the trees with armloads of brush and branches and dumping them by several fires in the center of the clearing. Others were heading back into the woods to scour up more firewood. All of them halted and stared, their voices dying away, as Lazlo checked his team and swung to the ground. They seemed to range in age roughly from four or five to their midteens; there must have been twenty or more of them.

Mark and Cissie were moving over to one of the fires where, Lazlo now perceived, there was another grown-up besides Mark. She was sitting on her heels, cradling a small girl on her lap, spooning gruel into the child's mouth as she made little clucking sounds of encouragement.

Mark added his armload of wood to a pile and turned to Lazlo and Hutch. "My sister, gentlemen, Miss Aretha Bly."

Although she had doubtless noted their arrival, the woman only now looked directly at them. She set the little girl on her feet gently and stood up.

She was a small, trim-bodied woman whose hair flamed red where it puffed from under her gray bonnet and, like many redheads, she was pale-skinned and freckled. Her face was plain and snub-nosed; her mouth was compressed but not severe. She looked almost frail in a flowing gray dress and a man's heavy Mackinaw coat. Although she hardly came to her brother's shoulder, she must be a dozen years his elder, and plainly she was in command here.

Lazlo pulled off his hat. "My name is Lazlo Kusik, ma'am. This is my friend, Hutch Prouter. We are crossing the mountains and came on your tracks a ways back. Mr. Bly thinks maybe we can get breakfast here."

"Indeed you may, sir. You're welcome to share what we have, although I'm afraid it's little enough."

She gave him a quick, strong handshake but didn't offer to do the same with Hutch, who hadn't bothered to remove his battered horsethief hat. Lazlo, who'd met all kinds in his roamings, placed her accent right away: like Mark's, it was that of a cultivated New Englander. Next to the forceful thrust of Aretha Bly's personality, her brother seemed gentle, almost anonymous. Her eyes were a calm bright blue like his, but hers held a kind of solemn rectitude that was almost pushy.

She handed the bowl of gruel to Cissie O'Halloran. "Cissie, take Abigail to the wagon and bundle her up warmly. Then try to coax her into eating a bit more."

"Yes'm, Miss Aretha." Cissie took the little girl by the hand and led her off.

Lazlo didn't think the small one looked well. Her face was pinched and pale, and she had a weak, unsteady walk, although she was well past babyhood. In addition, most of these children were poorly clad. Their clothing was threadbare, inadequate for the season, and much of it looked like oversize castoffs.

Charity kids, he thought abruptly. *That is it.*

"Please help yourselves, gentlemen. All of us have eaten." Miss Aretha motioned to the pots simmering by the fire, then turned to the watching children and clapped her hands together sharply. "Come now! You all have duties to perform. You know what they are."

As the kids dispersed, Lazlo and Hutch hunkered down, accepted the plates, tin cups, and forks handed to them by Mark, and served themselves gruel, sidemeat, and coffee from the pots. Hutch loaded his plate, but Lazlo, not wanting to impose on such a charity outfit as this obviously was, skimped on his helpings.

The two Blys crouched down on the other side of the fire, courteously saying nothing as their guests took the first edges off their appetites. Then Miss Aretha said, "I take it you gentlemen are making for Carson's Crossing?"

Hutch, wolfing down his food, didn't look at her or reply. Apparently he'd taken as instant a dislike to Miss Aretha as she obviously had to him. It was to Lazlo that she spoke.

"We are, ma'am. And you too?"

"Yes. Are you familiar with that place, Mr. Kusik?"

"Yes."

"A good place to live, would you say?"

Miss Aretha's face wore a peculiar look. Somehow it made Lazlo uneasy. "I would say that," he answered warily. "Do you mean to settle there?"

Carson's Crossing, where he had been more than once, lay in a fertile river valley to the west. It was in the center of a prosperous stock-raising region, and there was some mining and lumbering activity too. Not a bad place to be, if you could get across to it all right.

"In a manner of speaking." Miss Aretha spoke very crisply; her gaze was almost fierce. "I wonder, sir, if you have ever heard of the Children's Aid Society?"

"Uh, no, I have not."

"Well, it was founded some years ago by a Connecticut minister, the Reverend Charles Loring Brace. I suppose that you are not familiar either with the condition of homeless and abandoned children in the city of New York . . ."

Lazlo nodded a little wearily. "Yes'm. I know it very well."

"Oh?"

"I grew up there. At the Five Points on the Lower East Side."

"Ah! Then I hardly need tell you of the horrible circumstances in which these waifs exist. There are nearly ten thousand of them in the city of New York, Mr. Kusik. *Ten thousand!* Children living in squalor, filth, disease, misery . . . when they are permitted to live at all."

The light of a true zealot blazed in Miss Aretha's eyes now. Lazlo cleared his throat awkwardly. "Uh, yes. I believe—"

"That is not the worst. Unwanted babies by the hundreds are abandoned every year. Sometimes on the doorsteps of the well-to-do . . . but more often their pathetic little forms will be found dead and stiff in ashcans and back alleys—or floating in the East River. Many more—the *fortunate* homeless who survive—will eke out an existence in the alleys, eating bits of garbage from the streets, clothing their nakedness with rags . . . and of course filching and stealing!"

Miss Aretha's small fists clenched in her lap. "Boys, Mr. Kusik, become hardened criminals by the age of twelve or thirteen. Girls become women of—of the . . . female vagrants." She flushed, lowering her eyes. "I crave your pardon. I fear I am always carried away by the subject. It is all-absorbing to me. But you will be aware of the conditions I describe."

"I can say that I am—"

"Well, sir!—when the Reverend Brace founded the Children's Aid Society, it was with the intention of placing the orphaned and abandoned children of the slums with good families throughout New York and New England. Of course orphan asylums have been common in our eastern states since the 1830s, but the institutionalized care and raising of a child —Mr. Brace was certain—could never substitute for the virtues of a family upbringing. Genuine love and affection, along with the particular care and sound education that only a real home could provide, would not only alleviate a host of social problems, but it would also produce useful citizens.

"Indeed, his plan succeeded beyond all expectation! Not only has a sizable portion of the city's destitute youth been uplifted, their lives redeemed for gainful employment in farm and manufactory, but many have gone on to responsible positions in law, business, the professions. From potential menaces have been wrested worthwhile assets to society. Agents of our society are constantly in the field to call on applicants for foster parenthood and to verify their worth. They also follow closely the careers of those children whom their efforts have placed in foster homes. The evidence they have gathered to confirm the value of the society and its work is irrefutable!

"Well . . . after the initial success of his undertaking, Reverend Brace found that the demand for foster children was so widespread and the number of homeless children in the city of New York so great that he deemed it advisable to extend the society's activities westward—first, to such states of the Middle West as Michigan and Indiana. Again results were so encouraging that orphan trains were soon rolling toward Nebraska and other western states!"

Lazlo gave a polite, wary nod.

The woman's fervor was so genuine and passionate that he felt more than a little embarrassed. Also, sincere or not, all that she'd said sounded pretty much like a set speech. Not too surprising, at that. A lot of suffragettes, militant feminists, and the like were marching along the lecture circuit these days, even in remote parts of the West.

"My brother and I," Miss Aretha went on, "are in charge of this party of twenty orphans, under the auspices of the Children's Aid Society. Unfortunately our departure from New York was plagued by one delay after another. We were due in Carson's Crossing a full month ago. All was arranged many weeks in advance, you see. Every child in our party has the prospect of a good home, in town or on a ranch or farm."

Mark Bly cleared his throat—as if he too were a bit embarrassed by his sister's intensity. "We've come a long way, Mr. Kusik. By steamer on the Great Lakes and from Chicago by train. At Saba City, where rail connections terminate, we purchased several wagons and teams of mules, and from there came across the mountains as far as Bozetown."

Hutch gave a sardonic grunt. "You picked y'self a prime time for crossing these peaks." He picked up the scalding-hot coffeepot in a calloused hand that was impervious to heat and freshened his cup again. "Ain't no daisies growing up here this time o' year, son. What you ought'a done, you ought'a took the stage route to the south and west, around the mountains. It is a farther piece to go, but a heap safer. Ain't that right, Laz?"

Lazlo said, "Mmm," sort of noncommittally. His mind was ranging ahead, ferreting out what this situation might hold for him.

Miss Aretha looked directly at Hutch for the first time.

"We deemed it urgent," she said in a chilly voice, "due to unavoidable delays and the lateness of the season, to reach Carson's Crossing as soon as possible. We were told in Bozetown that in this mountain country winters are early arriving and that severe weather may be expected any day now."

"Yes'm." Hutch's mock-politeness was so elaborate that it bordered on insult. "That is more or less my point, ma'am. Ain't exactly the season for kiting across this here country, if you fetch my meaning, ma'am."

Miss Aretha clasped her finely shaped hands together in her lap, turning her gaze down at them, perhaps to offset modestly the tempered-steel flash of her eyes. "Mr. Kusik, perhaps *you* might give us credit for being greenhorns only up to a point. With winter coming on, naturally our first thought was to get our charges to their destination as quickly as possible. With that in mind, and in my admitted ignorance of the country, we chose the most direct route from Saba City to Carson's Crossing. None offered advice to the contrary . . . until we sought the advice of the officer of Bozetown camp, Mr. Friendly. By then, however, we had come that far. In any case, as I understand it, the southern route also holds its dangers. There has been Indian trouble along that way, and the stages are sometimes menaced by desperadoes. Also, may not winter conditions sometimes shut off those roads as well?"

Lazlo frowned at his empty plate. Unsure just what advice he wanted to give, he felt decidedly uncomfortable. "Well, once in a while. But mostly the stages get through all right. Maybe, with these wagons of yours, you can go on west through Trevo Pass. But when that ends, the trails over the Elks are very bad. They were made by animals and Indians. It will not be easy to get a wagon over them."

Too late, even as he spoke, Lazlo realized he'd erred.

Miss Aretha pounced on the point at once: "If the western

way across the peaks is so inadvisable, sir, why are you traversing it *with* a wagon?"

"I have my reasons," he said stiffly. "In any case, it does not matter much for me. If my wagon cannot get across, I will leave it and go on foot. I am in no danger of my life."

"Nor, in that event, are we. At least a half-dozen of our youngsters are older boys—large and husky enough to wrestle a wagon over the rough places on those terrible trails of yours. Should we be forced to abandon them, however, we would simply complete our journey on foot . . . although it would work a hardship on the younger children."

Her words tripped a trigger in Lazlo's mind.

His own heavy wagon might need just that kind of assistance. Those husky boys could be useful to him. Above all, in the company of the Blys and their wards, he would have around-the-clock protection against anything Hutch might be minded to try.

Then his conscience balked, sharp as a blade. It would be wrong to use these people that way. He shook his head almost angrily. "These mountains are nothing to take a bunch of kids across this time of year. You are crazy to try it. You'd do best to turn back to Saba City."

"Mr. Kusik!—"

"Sis," Mark interposed gently, "they can't know how serious our straits really are. Our funds have just about run out, Mr. Kusik. We can't afford to retrace our steps and then make a long and circuitous detour to reach Carson's Crossing. Our provisions are nearly gone—"

"And," Miss Aretha cut in crisply, "it will take only a few days—four at the most, Mr. Friendly estimated—to get across the peaks to the west, even allowing for ordinary difficulties. But to return to Saba City and then make a wide swing along the southern route would take the Lord knows how many days! Surely the gamble is worth it. We have enough provisions for several days—and the sooner we get to Carson's Crossing, obviously the less danger we face of being caught in an early blizzard."

"But some snow has fallen already. Why not turn back and lay over in Bozetown till spring?"

"We can't!" she said vehemently. "How would we feed and shelter twenty youngsters through a long winter? How could we risk holding the young lives entrusted to our care in that wild and lawless place all those months? Their souls already have been bruised by low passions to which I will not permit their being subjected any further. No, sir! We shall push on, and without delay!"

Lazlo gave a short, grim nod. She was determined to be insensible to any risk. These damned zealots usually were. But if she were bound to be a fool, why should he scruple at turning her stupidity to his advantage?

"Well," he began sourly, "since you're set on—"

He jerked and swore.

Something had stung him in the back of the neck, a smart pelletlike blow. He swung his head, rubbing his neck. A small boy in a man's ragged cutdown ulster stood a few yards away. He was bright-eyed and towheaded and held a peashooter in his grubby fist. He grinned impudently at Lazlo's glare.

"Cyrus—" Miss Aretha was sharply reproving. "You've been warned time and again! Mark, take that thing away from him."

The boy fled across the camp and into the trees. He trailed a taunting laugh. Mark loped after him.

"I'm sorry, Mr. Kusik. You were saying—?"

"Since you will go on no matter what," Lazlo said doggedly, "it would be good for us to throw in together. You could easily go astray on a wrong trail. Game trails and Indian trails—they twist all over and cross each other in the high passes. I know the best and shortest way . . ."

"Me too," chimed in Hutch. "Reckon you could use both our services, Miss Bly, ma'am."

Hutch's manner had changed abruptly. He was grinning almost handsomely as he waggled his shaggy head up and down.

Miss Aretha's manner softened perceptibly. She looked from one to the other. "That is a generous offer. I am grateful to both of you . . ."

CHAPTER 11

The wagons moved out within the hour. By now a weak diffusion of daylight filled the broad stretch of the pass, although the sun never showed on the slate-banded horizon. But the sheen of new snow picked up what light there was and clearly etched the whole landscape.

Lazlo took the lead, breaking track for the Blys' three wagons.

The land ahead of them still rolled flat and even, so that in places the snow had drifted enough to obscure the faint trail. Hutch tramped beside or behind Lazlo's wagon, sometimes well behind it. Lazlo knew he was inspecting the wheel tracks again, comparing them to those of the other wagons.

I will still have to keep an eye on him. But now it will be easier.

After a while, wanting to stretch his legs, Lazlo asked Hutch to take over the driving chore. Dropping back a little along the line of wagons, he grimly noted that the Blys' larger and, on the face of it, more heavily loaded wagons left far lighter wheel indentations than his own.

If Hutch hadn't been reasonably sure before, he was now.

The kids, anyway, were having a great time with the moist, crunchy snow. A few of the youngest, and a couple of really sickly ones, rode in the wagons, but most of the boys and girls were cavorting around the slow-moving vehicles, packing and flinging snowballs, their childish cries ringing in the frosty stillness. Miss Aretha made a half-hearted effort to shush them, but presently, smiling and shaking her head, she gave it up. Who could suppress a bunch of kids full of coltish energies and still wearing an early-morning edge?

Miss Aretha was handling the team behind Lazlo's with a brisk, no-nonsense competence; Mark was on the driver's seat of the next in line; a husky fifteen-year-old named Tim brought up the rear.

Lazlo was tramping alongside Mark's wagon, idly chatting with him, when a snowball whizzed past his head, missing it by a couple of inches. He turned in time to catch a glimpse of Cyrus disappearing around the tailgate with a thumb-to-nose "*Nyaaah!*"

Grinning, Mark said, "He likes you. I can tell. Better be on your guard. I didn't get that peashooter away from him. Couldn't catch him."

"That does not surprise me," Lazlo said dourly.

"I imagine not. I've a feeling, Mr. Kusik, that you have no great opinion of us—or our mission. We must impress you as a pair of errant and hare-brained do-gooders. And all-around incompetents—eh?"

"I would not say that."

Lazlo was merely being polite.

In fact, probing back into his memory, he realized that he *had* heard of the Children's Aid Society before. It had already been operating on New York's Lower East Side when he was a kid. But although he and his mother had known the worst kind of poverty, she had lived till he was in his late teens. By then a brawny youth well able to take care of himself, he'd had no use for social services. That was when he'd departed for the Middle West, to spend the years of his young manhood following the harvest crews. He knew as well as anyone how the poor of New York festered out their lives in the dreary stews of their ghettoes. But he'd paid his own debts all his life, never asking any assistance outside of his own resources.

Maybe he wasn't being fair. But experience hadn't equipped him to think in any other terms. Possibly the kids *would* be better off out here in God's clean country . . . but life in the West was rough and raw, any way you tried to live it. And people were disappointingly the same any place you found them. That was the cynic's definition, Lazlo supposed, but to him it seemed right on the head. It would be a waste of time

telling young Mark that, though. Or that rock-ribbed sister of
his.

He expressed his thoughts aloud more obliquely: "What I
wonder is why a pair like you got into this kind of work. You
are gently bred, you and your sister."

"You might say that," Mark said affably. " 'Retha and I
were born into fairly comfortable circumstances, as children of
a Boston mercantile merchant. But our mother died bearing
me, and our father followed her when I was five and 'Retha
was seventeen. We were farmed out to relatives much less well
off, and on 'Retha fell much of the burden of seeing to my upbringing and education. It marked both of us, I suppose. Too,
we're Quakers. It seemed natural for us to take up charitable
work, at first for the Society of Friends, later for Reverend
Brace's Society."

"She is a strong-willed woman, your sister."

"Mmm. Well, *I* tried to talk her out of this mountain crossing, Mr. Kusik. But she was adamant."

"You would be in a pretty pickle if I had not come along,"
Lazlo said bluntly. "Didn't your sister think of hiring a guide?"

"Oh, certainly. In fact we approached—with Marshal
Friendly's guidance—a number of men in Bozetown. All
thought we were crazy. None would consent to undertake the
job for as little as we could afford to offer—except for a couple of men 'Retha didn't like the look of."

Lazlo's grunt held a tinge of contempt. "So. And if you
didn't get caught in a blizzard, still you might get good and lost
and then starve or freeze up there. Did anyone think of that?"

Mark flushed a little. "Well, we have a good compass.
'Retha thought that with its aid we couldn't go far astray. After
all, Carson's Crossing is almost exactly due west . . . isn't it?"

Sweet God Almighty, Lazlo groaned inwardly.

He inspected the sky above the saw-toothed range ahead
with grim care. Any frail sign of how the weather might turn
over the next few days would be a help. So far he could tell
nothing. The temperature was crisp but not too cold. If it went
way up, fine. If it hung steady, though, more snow might fall.

For a lone husky man making his way across the peaks, it

would not matter. But these kids—some of them looked so puny and sickish. Too much snow or too much cold: either could spell disaster. Then . . . another Donner party? A party of *children?* Lazlo shut his mind against the thought. Hell, a man had forebodings all the time. Almost always they came to nothing.

What really bothered him was that he was actually starting to feel concerned about this passel of damn fool innocents.

* * *

The wagons rolled steadily west through a long day. By first dark they'd crossed the last of the flatlands and the end of Trevo Pass. Beyond lay the imposing arm of mountains, and in its foothills by a rushing stream they made camp. Tomorrow the real ordeal would begin.

The mules were unhitched, watered, and fed. The children gathered dead brush, and roaring fires were built up. Everyone huddled around them and thawed out while Miss Aretha, bustling about and seeming to be everywhere at once, got preparations for the evening meal underway. Her mouth was set in a tight angry line all the while, and Lazlo knew why.

Hutch Prouter's upswing of mood hadn't lasted long. For most of the day he'd been dipping into his store of gin and whiskey. Now he shuffled around the camp like a blubbery baboon, cursing and muttering to himself, openly leering at Cissie and other young girls.

Maybe I will have to put him down after all, Lazlo thought narrowly. *Best, though, to say or do nothing right now; it might only worsen matters.*

Supper was dished up, and everyone was served a portion. Miss Aretha motioned them all to gather around a central fire, and there, in a primitive flicker of light that seemed a kind of brave beacon against the darkness all around, she bowed her head and led a prayer of thanksgiving. The children bowed their heads too, the boys pulling off their ragged caps.

Miss Aretha looked up and shot a meaningful glance at Lazlo. In belated realization, he yanked off his hat and gave Hutch, glaze-eyed and swaying at his side, a hard nudge.

Hutch, however, not only refused to doff his hat, he barely

touched his meager serving of supper. It wasn't like him, but Lazlo, thinking that Hutch had drunk too much to be very hungry, gave it only a passing thought. He paid little attention when Hutch wobbled off into the darkness as Miss Aretha led the children in singing "Shall We Gather at the River?" Likely he was going off to be sick, or to relieve himself, or to swill down more booze; whichever, he would doubtless pass out before long.

Then, unbidden, a thought struck Lazlo. He left the group by the fire, swiftly following Hutch toward the south edge of the camp, where his wagon was.

As he'd expected, he found Hutch there. But he was not engaged in digging out another bottle. Instead Hutch was bent down, muttering to himself in a fierce, slurred undertone as he peered at the wagon's tailgate and underside.

So, Lazlo thought coldly, *now he is starting to think. With all the booze in him, he is starting to think.*

"You are all right, Hutch? Eh?"

Hutch straightened up with a jerk. In the dim reach of firelight, his bearded face seemed as malignant as a troll's. He strained out a laugh through his big teeth.

"Oh. Sure, little pard. Fine as frog's hair. Felt a mite sickish back there, was all."

"I thought that might be it," Lazlo said mildly. "I do not think this Aretha Bly takes very kindly to you, Hutch."

"That is God's own truth." Hutch belched, swaying tubbily. "Goddamn high-hat bitch," he rumbled. "Where'n hell does she get off, looking at me like I was a goddamn pig?"

If you look like a pig and act like a pig, you will be taken for one, Lazlo felt like saying but didn't. "Come, Hutch. They are gentlefolk, these Blys, and we are too rough for them. You're tired, eh? Get some sleep, why don't you?"

"Yeah," Hutch said groggily. "Mebbe that is what I need some of. Sleep."

Lazlo got Hutch's blankets out of the wagon and spread them out close by, then supported the big man's sagging weight as he maneuvered him over to the blankets. Hutch toppled into them with a sodden grunt.

"You're a honest-to-Christ nice fella, Laz," he groaned, pulling the blankets around him. "Gonna side with you all the way, li'l pard. You believe it. Yessir. Alla way . . ."

That was Lazlo's biggest worry. But he thrust it and all other worries to the back of his mind. He needed sleep too. He carried his own soogans off a little ways, spread them out, and rolled into them. He'd just composed himself for sleep when a smarting blow on his face brought him half-upright, his heart pounding.

The faint sound of boyish laughter came from the fringe of the forest. Lazlo knew the voice. Fleetingly he saw the small dark form of Cyrus vanish into the woods. He felt something reposing in the front socket of his collarbone. He rolled it between his fingers, knowing sight unseen what it was. A dry, hard, wrinkled pea.

Lazlo swore once and loudly in the badly remembered tongue of his parents. Even as he was running over sadistic possibilities of how he might satisfactorily get back at the little bastard, his thoughts broke apart and threaded away. He slipped into the sleep of complete exhaustion.

* * *

It didn't last long—an hour or maybe less.

At first the sounds dripped like slow strands of molasses into the deep well of his slumber. Then they pulled him upward and outward toward a muddy awareness. Sounds of . . . *breaking glass?*

The giant roar of a man's voice shook him completely awake. Lazlo sat bolt upright in his blankets, blinking his eyes, listening. Then he scrambled to his feet, hand closing over his rifle, and stumbled toward the sounds.

He hadn't far to go. Light from the fire picked out the scene in hard relief. He pulled to a stop, hands tight around his rifle but not bringing it to bear.

Miss Aretha stood by the side of his wagon, clutching a hand ax. At her feet lay a crumpled bundle that he recognized as Hutch's sack of possibles. It glistened with a dark spreading wetness. Mark was beside her, his face pale in the orange glow. They were confronting Hutch like a pair of bantams. He stood a few yards from them, his mighty shoulders drawn up and his great hands fisting and unfisting at his sides. Lazlo could see his bearded face only in quarter-profile, but in the dancing light it looked mean as hell. He appeared ready to kill.

The children were gathering around too, but at a safe distance. They looked frightened, confused, dismayed. Miss Aretha's small face wore a quiet look of iron. Mark appeared less sure of himself, but just as determined as his sister.

Lazlo stepped into the space between Hutch and the Blys. "What is going on?"

"That tony goddamn bitch!" Hutch bellowed. "Ask her! Ask her what she went and done."

Lazlo glanced at Miss Aretha. She stood very stiff and straight, her chin up. "Mr. Prouter," she said icily, "has given us no opportunity to explain. I fear, even so, that he will not accept the explanation. Our children, Mr. Kusik, have gotten into the liquor your friend so providentially packed along."

Lazlo said tonelessly, "The kids?"

"Exactly. The kids. I noticed, some minutes ago, that several of the boys were behaving strangely. And then I realized why. They were drunk!"

Her eyes blazed with a kind of blue fire. In that moment, just passingly, Lazlo wondered why he'd ever thought of this small woman as plain. She might not even be pretty. But plain? Never.

"And you thought—"

"Not right away. But I wasn't long arriving at the answer. What else could it be? There is no liquor among our supplies, not even for medicinal purposes. We've taken especial pains to ensure as much. So the liquor they found and consumed could only have been among your supplies, sir, or"—the full venom of her look pounced on Hutch—"*his.*"

"Didn't give her no call to get out that goddamn hatchet o' hers and bust up my cache o' redeye," Hutch rumbled. He lifted his big hands, palms up, fingers curling into thick hooks. "Now you get clear out o' the way, little pard. I got me some damage to do . . ."

"That is enough." Lazlo wanted only to keep the peace, but

he swung up his rifle to lay emphasis on the order. He looked at Aretha Bly. "What kind of kids are these, to go into things belonging to a man? And then drink themselves drunk on his booze?"

"*You* ask me that, Mr. Kusik?" Her blue-fire eyes impaled him. "You who claim you grew up at the Five Points?"

"Well, I did. But—"

"Then my God, sir! Why question the fact? Surely you're aware that many of these slum children, through no fault of their own, are addicted to monstrous vices. Not the least of which is *drinking gin!*"

Lazlo dipped his head up and down, wearily. "Something of the sort was known to me."

"Well, sir! If you can still fault my reason for appropriating and 'smashing this . . . this fellow's supply of it, you're considerably less than the man I'd taken you to be."

Miss Aretha stood with arms folded, her stare fierce and imperious.

What she didn't understand was that Hutch too was an addict and that cutting him off from his beloved hooch, suddenly and cold turkey, had turned him into an ugly and dangerous brute. One who had to be placated—somehow. Or stopped dead in his tracks.

"What is done is done, Hutch," he said mildly. "In three days, maybe, we will be across the peaks. Then I'll buy you out a whole saloon. How is that?"

"Three days . . ." Flamelight raked Hutch's eyes with a red heat. "I could walk back to Bozetown a heap quicker."

"That is up to you. Do what you must."

"I'll tell you what you best do, boy. Move away."

Hutch took a lumbering step forward. Lazlo leveled the rifle on his chest. Hutch came to a stop, but his face was working maniacally.

"You want to stop me, Laz boy, you better use that straightway and make your first shot count. Won't be no time for a second, as before that I will have you busted in two."

"You will make me kill you?"

"Come to that, I will." Hutch's voice was guttural and implacable. "You don't mix in this now. Step off."

Lazlo's gaze swept the ground and lighted on a fallen branch. He walked over to it, still holding his rifle pointed one-handed, and bent to close a hand on it. He set a foot on the branch, broke off the thick butt end, and then, experimentally, swung it back and forth. It would do.

He walked over to Mark Bly and handed him the rifle. "You know how to use this?"

"Yes. But—"

"If I lose, shoot him."

The calm order clearly shocked Mark; even his rock-ribbed sister paled a little. What in hell did they think they'd bought into, breaking up a drunk's liquor cache? A tea party, maybe?

Lazlo did not want to shoot Hutch. He still had the raw taste of one man's recent death at his hands.

With time to take a good aim, he could shoot to cripple, not kill. But it was too easy for a man to die even of a crippling wound, given what medical care he could expect in this country—usually none. Lazlo had seen it happen too often.

Men did not die of beatings so often. If he could fetch Hutch a sound beating, it might head off worse. He didn't press the thought of how much chance he'd stand against Hutch's bearlike bigness and sheer strength.

Go ahead and do it; that is all. If you can.

Hutch grunted and belched and showed his big teeth. It might have been a grin. He waited, hands loose at his sides now.

Would the liquor he'd taken slow him? Lazlo hoped so. He knew how fast Hutch could move in spite of his sway-bellied bulk. If he ever got those huge hands on a man of ordinary size, God help that man.

Don't give him any time to think about it!

Hutch might be fast on his feet, but how quick of wit was he?

Lazlo rushed in, raising his club two-handed above his head. Hutch's fist pulled back. At the last moment, Lazlo swerved aside, evading the mighty swing Hutch intended for his head. He brought the club down in a crushing blow on Hutch's extended arm.

It had enough force to break bones. Even Hutch's. But the big man's arm was corded with resilient muscle that padded the impact. Even so, the pain made Hutch stagger backward, his eyes glazed with shock.

Lazlo whirled in two quick steps around and slightly behind the big man, pivoting on his heel. Another two-handed swing of his wood billet, this time in a horizontal arc, slammed Hutch across the kidneys.

Hutch howled and dropped to his hands and knees. Lazlo took a sideward step to get Hutch's thick knob of a skull squarely in range and raised the club again. Now he had time for a full overhead swing that would pound Hutch into oblivion. It would be over that swiftly—that easily.

He hadn't reckoned quite enough with Hutch's stamina and cunning. On his hands and knees, wagging his head back and forth as if to clear it, Hutch suddenly shot out a long arm. He grabbed Lazlo by the ankle and yanked. Lazlo's feet shot from under him, dumping him flat on his back.

Hutch kept a bruisingly powerful hold on Lazlo's ankle as he floundered forward to get the final grip he needed. His face was discolored with pain and whiskey and triumph as he got his knees under him, free arm crooked at an angle that would protect his head against another swing of the club.

Lazlo kicked futilely at Hutch with his other leg. His leverage was bad; Hutch easily blocked the awkward kicks. Hutch was raised above him now, teeth bared with a feral and murderous expectancy.

"Go on, little pard," he husked, "try'n hit me—"

Something else hit him.

Lazlo didn't see what, but it caught Hutch in the region of his right ear. He let out a high-pitched yowl and clapped a hand to his temple. In the same moment he swung his head sideways, not yowling now.

He was bellowing. Shouting imprecations at a small boy with a peashooter.

Cyrus, bless him!

It gave Lazlo the momentary opening he needed. Hutch's arm had dropped, leaving his bearded head wide open. For Lazlo, it was a bad position from which to administer a *coup de grace;* flat on his back, Hutch's weight half-pinning him, and damned little room in which to swing a club.

Still he tried. He swung with all his strength.

The billet broke in half on Hutch's thick skull. The blow would have laid out a lesser man for hours. Hutch just swayed above him, glassy-eyed and stunned. Lazlo followed up fast— with a fist still wrapped around the billet stub. The punch had enough power to swivel Hutch's head, forcing an explosive grunt from him.

Slowly then, he toppled sideways.

Lazlo heaved off Hutch's weight and climbed to his feet. He limped over to Mark, took the rifle from him, and went back to Hutch, who was climbing laboriously to his knees.

Lazlo put the rifle muzzle to the back of Hutch's head.

"Now, Hutch," he said between his teeth, "you have got me just about mad enough to blow out your brains. So don't tempt me. Get your stuff and clear out of here. And mind . . . if I find you dogging my trail again, I will not talk anymore." A long pause. "What I will do is, I will shoot you on sight."

Hutch rubbed a hand over his face and looked at it, smeared bright with his blood. Finally he spoke, "You have said it all, little pard," followed by a chest-deep chuckle.

The liquor had washed out of Hutch's voice. It was strained and wicked. He turned his head enough for Lazlo to see the grinning grimace that shaped his fleshy face so that somehow it seemed as gauntly cruel as a skull.

"I will be dogging you right enough. Only you won't noways see me when I come. Time you do, it will be way too late. That is God's own truth."

CHAPTER 12

Arms folded on the table, Laban Ruddy eyed the man sitting across from him with a frustrated swell of anger that he was careful not to let show. You could smooth-talk a man like Creed Jacks all day and all night, Laban was bitterly convinced, and never dent his dry composure.

Creed Jacks looked like anything but a man whose reputation with a gun had run ahead of him even to this remote corner of the West. He was slight of build, under medium height, with a voice so whisper-soft that you had to cock your head to make out what he said.

Everything about him seemed sort of nondescript and washed-out. The gray that streaked his hair was almost imperceptible against its dead paleness. His eyes were of no particular color. He might have been anywhere from thirty-five to fifty-five. Anyone trying to describe him after once seeing him, Laban thought, would have a hard time remembering how he looked.

A man would remember his clothes, no doubt. Creed Jacks wore fine black broadcloth of a conservative cut, tailored to his slight frame, along with a pearl-gray Stetson and a handsome sheepskin coat. A diamond stickpin glittered in his cravat. Quiet and tasteful and expensive: the costume of a man used to having plenty of money and spending it in a casual but never flashy way. God knew what whim or idle purpose had brought him to this remote gold camp.

One thing was sure: he was a man utterly sure of himself, utterly unconcerned about anything or anyone else, unless they got in his way or could be used to his advantage. When Laban had approached the table where Creed Jacks sat alone and asked if he might join him, Jacks had nodded courteously even while his pallid gaze briefly and impersonally sized up Laban and then dismissed him.

Though irked, Laban had bought Jacks a drink and then laid it all out for him in the plainest terms, underpitching his voice against the raucous, smoky din of Red Mike's saloon.

* * *

For two days and nights Laban Ruddy, his remaining nephew, and Robert Topbear had kept a watch on the road to Saba City. They'd taken up positions on the flanks of two high ridges that formed part of the pass through which the road ran, about a half-mile east from Bozetown.

It was a cold, cramped, and tedious vigil. And to Laban's disgust, Lazlo Kusik had failed to show up.

This had puzzled him. All signs had indicated that Kusik intended to pull out soon. If he did, they'd be sure to spot his slow-moving wagon by keeping a watch on the road to Saba City. What had gone wrong? Had the hunky changed his mind? Surely he'd anticipated that Laban and his boys would get hold of more guns and make another try at him. With that thought, Laban had sent Robert Topbear to reconnoiter Lazlo's claim camp. Returning a couple of hours later, Topbear had reported that the camp was deserted. Kusik, his wagon, and all his belongings were gone.

But *where?* Topbear couldn't say. Snow had fallen, but the wind had drifted over any tracks.

The question fed Laban's growing angry bafflement. He'd been told back in Saba City that the only way in or out of the Mad Mule River Valley by wagon was through the deep pass that ran east between folded ridges and flanking mountains all the way to Saba City. What could they do but keep watching it?

Finally, after another fruitless day and night of chilly vigil on a ridgeside, Laban, viciously sober and out of whiskey, had left Bije and Robert Topbear on watch and tramped back to Bozetown where he could pick up more liquor and, just maybe, some trifles of information that would put him on the right scent.

Engaging the bartender at Red Mike's in talk, Laban had asked first about Kusik's ally, Hutch Prouter. He might get a line on Kusik's whereabouts through Prouter. Informed that Prouter's camp lay on the Mad Mule a little way above Kusik's, Laban decided to try his luck there. Maybe—

Then, right out of the blue, the barkeep said idly, "Say, you see that fella over in the corner drinking by hisself? Know who he is?"

Laban gave the man an indifferent glance. "No, I don't."

"Creed Jacks, that is. Used to see him a lot when I was tending bar at the Silver Eagle, way down in Tombstone. He was mixed up with Sheriff Behan and that Clanton crowd against Earp 'n' his brothers—"

Laban cut in, "I've heard of him," and eyed the slight, unimpressive man with a fresh interest.

Creed Jacks. A man deadly with a gun. That, Laban Ruddy was now convinced, was what he needed more than anything. More even than good luck or a sound lead on Kusik and Prouter.

Truth to tell, much as he was set on tracking down Lazlo Kusik, the fellow had Laban Ruddy more than a little spooked. There was an edge of danger in Kusik. You could feel it, by God, under that quiet hunky manner of his. He'd already demonstrated that he was a mean customer to tangle with. That friend of his, Prouter, wasn't to be taken lightly either.

If they tackled Kusik again, it had to be a sure thing.

Laban himself was a stranger to violence and firearms. So were Bije and Robert Topbear. Stella's prowess with a rifle might have been turned to good use, but Stella was less concerned with getting back at the man who'd slain her cousin Ab than with caring for her sister Myra Mae, who'd come down with another of her periodic bouts of severe coughing. So the two girls had remained in the camp on Humbug Flat.

Creed Jacks was a killer. His worn-handled Colt in its worn holster, the skirt of his coat pushed back to keep the butt clear, was the only outward sign of it. Only his reputation was right out front for anyone to see. It preceded him wherever he went.

The problem was that Creed Jacks hadn't bought any of Laban's pitch.

He'd listened to Laban's story patiently and politely, staring with show-nothing eyes at his glass of whiskey on the table between them, twirling it gently between his fingers. When Laban was done, Creed Jacks had said mildly, "Well now, sir, let's look at what we have got here. Way I understand it, you have a mere pittance in your poke. Hardly enough to make it worth my while to waste a twitch of my little finger on your behalf."

"I told you—"

"What you've told me," Creed Jacks went on, "is that you assume, on a basis of far from conclusive evidence, that a certain hunky miner has made himself a quite lucrative strike. In toto, Mr. Ruddy, what you've offered me in support of that contention is considerably less than convincing."

"Mr. Jacks . . ."

Sweat damped Laban's face. He was feeling a need for support that verged on desperation. And he wanted that support from Creed Jacks. "You're a gambler, I have heard. Listen then. Here's a gamble worth the taking. Side with me in this, and I guarantee you'll have your hands on half of whatever Kusik's strike amounts to. Even at a gamble, sir, that should prove to be considerable."

Creed Jacks remained politely smiling and wearily skeptical. "I am a cynical man, Mr. Ruddy. In my time I have heard about every story under the sun. I do not believe in purple cows. Nor pigs in pokes."

That was where the matter rested for the next twenty minutes, during which Laban wracked his brain for all the arguments he could summon from a lifetime of experience at snake-oil persuasion, none of it to any effect.

Creed Jacks nursed along the whiskey Laban had bought him and politely refused to drink up so that Laban could buy him another. He replied to anything Laban said with a murmured word or so, and his gaze was faraway.

Laban was about ready to give up when, casting an idle glance around the room, he saw a big man push his way through the swing doors on the far side of the dim, noisy, log-walled room.

It was Hutch Prouter. The sight of him did nothing to improve Laban's state of mind.

Hutch bellied his way over to the bar and brought a big fist crashing down on it. He roared that he wanted a bottle, *goddammit!*—and his stentorian bellow caused the hubbub in Red Mike's to ebb momentarily into silence. Prouter got his bottle, paid for it, and tipped it to his mouth. His head went back; his Adam's apple bobbed for a quarter-minute. When he lowered the bottle and swiped a hairy hand across his mouth, the bottle was a third empty.

Prouter's gaze moved across the crowd and stopped on Laban Ruddy. Laban felt his innards squeeze up under Hutch's stare. A moment later they crumpled even tighter as Prouter shoved away from the bar and started across the room toward him.

Judas Priest in a jug! Laban thought wildly. He sat in a paralyzed panic that increased with a closer sight of Prouter's face.

Before, the fellow had seemed as jovial as a clown. Hadn't appeared very temper-tight even when he'd helped Kusik overcome Laban and the boys. But now his broad face wore as purely mean and ugly a look as Laban had ever seen.

My God, what does he mean to do!

All Prouter did was grab the third chair at the table in a hamlike hand, yank it out, and slack heavily into it.

"You 'n' me," he growled at Laban, "got medicine to make. Best hear me out."

Prouter paused for another belt of liquor. He set the bottle gently down, and it was half-empty now. Laban, himself a steady but slow drinker, felt a proper awe. Prodigious feats of "putting it away" were nothing unusual in a mining camp, but he'd never seen the like of this.

A half-quart of booze had done nothing to soften whatever devil was working in Prouter. His face was craggy with temper, and now Laban noticed the crusted scab of blood that had dried on his temple.

"Who's he?" Prouter motioned curtly at Creed Jacks, who was giving him a bemused, mildly interested stare.

Laban performed the introductions.

"Heerd o' you," Prouter told Jacks and leaned his massive forearms on the table. "I got som'at to tell you, Ruddy. 'Bout Laz Kusik and a mess o' gold." He jerked a thumb at Creed Jacks. "He 'ith you? Want him to hear this or not?"

Laban hesitated, his brain working with a swift sure instinct. Whatever Prouter was on the peck about, his wrath wasn't directed at Laban Ruddy. "Why not? Say what you want to."

In less than five minutes, even allowing for Laban's own excited interjection of questions as he sought clarification on details of what Hutch told him, the situation was clear.

When Hutch paused at last, taking another hefty pull at his bottle, Laban shuttled his gaze to Creed Jacks. He looked at ease, leaning back in his chair and smiling very faintly. His eyes no longer seemed colorless. They held the cold gray sheen of half-thawed ice.

"What you told me before," he murmured, "commences to interest me, *Colonel* Ruddy."

It ought to. Hutch Prouter had practically handed them on a platter a convincing affirmation of Laban's own arguments, along with a plan of operation. Out of what Hutch had said, the few things of importance could quickly be isolated: Prouter had reason to be sure of Kusik's cache of gold and where it was hidden. The falling-out between Prouter and Kusik had left Hutch in a seething rage—as ready as Laban himself to kill for revenge and money.

Best of all, he could guide them right to where Kusik was. All they'd need to implement the plan was some saddle mounts that could be bought or rented from the livery barn.

Not stirring from his slack position, Jacks reached out and picked up Hutch's bottle, saying genially, "Mr. Prouter, I hope you didn't intend to drink this up all by yourself. After all . . ." He filled his and Laban's glasses from the bottle and handed it back to Hutch. "I think the occasion calls for a toast to what appears a most promising partnership. Gentlemen— here's to ill-gotten gains. And a three-way split on them."

CHAPTER 13

After Hutch's departure, Lazlo got a night's sound sleep, for which he was grateful. Mark and a couple of the older boys took turns on guard duty, just in case. Lazlo had inspected the weapons owned by the party. These consisted of a battered Winchester and a vintage Hawken rifle much like the one of which he'd relieved Hutch, along with Hutch's old Walker Colt.

Weaponless, Hutch wasn't likely to sneak back. Possibly he could rearm himself in Bozetown and then overtake their slow wagons on foot. But one man shouldn't pose much of a danger as long as they stayed on their guard.

Lazlo's biggest worry now was nature's own temper.

Throughout the next day of climbing through the foothills and into the high passes, the weather held steady. They made pretty fair time. Wherever the going was rough for wagons and mules, the combined young muscles of boys and girls alike were enough to wrestle the wagons across.

It was a long and grueling day. Everyone was wrung out, literally exhausted, when the early darkness of late fall forced a halt. They had covered, Lazlo estimated, about half the distance. If he got them on all the right trails, and barring accidents or bad weather or other obstructions, they should be across the worst of it in another two days or less.

Keep your fingers crossed.

By midmorning of the next day, he had the sinking knowledge that it would take a lot more than crossed fingers to bring them safely through. The sky beyond the peaks was a raw gray sludge. Fierce churnings of wind tumbled the clouds ahead of them like masses of dirty fleece. Before long they'd be directly overhead. There would be no nooning today. They must push on quickly, covering as much distance as possible before the storm hit.

The first flakes of snow whirled down as light as dust. The snowfall picked up rapidly in an hour or so, and then what Lazlo had feared was confirmed: This wouldn't be another light snowfall. They were pointed into the teeth of a full-fledged blizzard.

It struck almost abruptly and with a blinding ferocity that cut off the world all around. It didn't merely destroy visibility; it wiped out a person's sense of direction and almost knocked him off his feet.

Lazlo had already prepared the Blys, and they were quick to follow his direction. The wagons were pulled into a square, and everyone huddled in its center, blankets clutched around them, using one another for windbreaks and warmth. There was little talk because you had to yell to be heard. The howling wind snatched ordinary speech away in dim tatters . . .

* * *

It was nearly midnight when the storm began to let up.

Lazlo was the first to break out of the shroud of snow that covered him. He shrugged free of his crusted blankets, stood up, and looked around. He couldn't make out much in the darkness and slackening fall of flakes. He tramped around, testing the depth of fallen snow. Not as bad as he'd feared, but deep enough to impede their progress. Up ahead, for all he knew, it might be too heavily drifted for wagons to buck through. Or the maze of trails might be obscured enough to give him the devil's own time trying not to lead them on a wrong turn.

He didn't say his doubts aloud. Not right then.

As the snow and wind continued to die off, Miss Aretha gave the kids orders: Gather wood (not easy to scour up at this height, almost above the timberline), get the fires going and a supper cooking, and tend the needs of the younger or ailing children first. As always, her calm crisp manner and her undiminished store of energy got into everyone else. After the camp was bedded down, the kids nestled in the wagons, Lazlo and Mark and Miss Aretha remained by one of the fires, sitting on their heels and sipping coffee.

"Well, Mr. Kusik," Aretha Bly said with a wry smile, "you said we were crazy to attempt a crossing this time of year. I am bound to confess you were probably right."

Lazlo sipped the dregs of his coffee. "It could be. But we've come this far. We have crossed most of the way. Now we must keep on. It may be bad ahead, but it could be just as bad behind, after this blizzard. We don't know."

"We don't, do we? I believe I told you that even if our wagons were marooned up here, we could continue on foot. We can, of course. But . . . some of the children are not in the best of health. And going through snowdrifts, it will take longer than we'd thought. Can we all make it, even so? What do you think?"

Lazlo felt only a sour trace of satisfaction in having this iron-willed woman defer to his opinion. Just now his thoughts revolved around his private dilemma. If the passes were closed off to wagons, he might lose the biggest gamble of his life. At the least, he'd be forced to abandon his gold till spring opened the high trails once more. That could be six months from now. The idea of waiting that long fretted him.

Worse: Hutch knew he'd come this way. If, later, Hutch followed up the trail and found the abandoned wagon, he would tear it apart to verify what he suspected and then would make his own plans for getting the cargo out. He would have other plans, too—for nailing up Lazlo's hide. Hutch was not stupid. He would lay those plans with care.

I have got to get through now, Lazlo thought doggedly. *There can be no waiting.*

Unwilling to show the Blys these thoughts, he let the cold anger he felt roughen his voice: "I think we better try to get across. We better try like hell . . . *now.*"

Miss Aretha colored. The way her blue eyes sparked was neither prim nor zealous. Mark Bly cleared his throat and unfolded his lanky frame, getting to his feet. "Um, think I'll turn in now, sis. G'night. Night, Mr. Kusik."

The crunch of his boots died away in the dark. Miss Aretha

stared at the fire and said, "I do not require coarse-grained sarcasm in reply to a simple question, Mr. Kusik. I have already confessed my fault. What more would you have me say?"

"I am sorry," he said lamely. "I was thinking . . ."

"Yes?"

"Of something else."

"Oh."

A little enigmatic smile brushed her lips. She rose and walked over to a tall snow-covered rock. Laying a mittened hand on it, she tipped back her head as if listening to the moan of wind from the craggy heights above.

"How much of a fool have I been, Mr. Kusik?"

Lazlo lifted one shoulder in a mild shrug. "It is as you have said. If we're shut off, we can go ahead on foot. But it will take much longer, and some of these kids of yours are not in such good condition. Also, if the trails are drifted, I could lose my way. None of it can be helped. We have come most of the way, and now we must go on. The trails in back of us are blown over too, now. If it's a choice between going on and turning back . . ."

"Of course," she murmured, "we must go on. You're kind not to say I'm a fool woman."

"If you are a fool, I do not think it has to do with being a woman."

Miss Aretha laughed, shortly and sharply. "What an arch flatterer you are, sir!" Her jaw clenched; she looked away from him. "I have taken a number of wrong turns in my life. Perhaps this was just another."

"Wrong turns? I cannot see you taking even one."

"More than a few, I fear. Some years ago I was denounced at a meeting of the Society of Friends . . . for defending the feminist doctrines of Susan B. Anthony and Elizabeth Cady Stanton. That was when I quit their society and took up with the Reverend Brace's. Mark followed my lead, even as he wryly observed that no matter what I do, I'll always need a cause. One cause or another to follow. Oh well . . ." Her laugh was quiet and self-deprecating. "I suppose I just take too much on myself. For years—being a mere woman—I was relegated to all kinds of minor tasks for the Children's Aid Society. Now, finally, I've been given an assignment of some responsibility. I am the first woman to be put in charge of shepherding a party of orphans to their new homes in the West." She bit her lip and shook her head. "Now . . . oh Lord."

It was, Lazlo realized, a rare moment of weakness in a woman like this. It embarrassed him. He had been a fighter all his life, and he hated to see a feeling of failure in anyone. But it showed in a woman like Aretha Bly, with all her spirit and courage, far more obtusely than in most.

Not knowing quite what to say, he got to his feet and walked over to her. "Listen, how have you done so bad?"

"How have I *not?*" She swiped a mitten across her nose. "I started out so full of self-assurance—with no understanding of what I'd have to face. What a fool I was!"

"No. It is a mood you are in. That passes."

"Sir, I have made *little* mistakes along the way. But pride can suffer those. This one might cost some children their lives. Do you think—"

"What I think," he broke in roughly, "is that you are one hell of a woman, and you do not seem to know it. Or is that, also, too coarse?"

"I don't think so." She was still-faced, head tipped back a little. Somehow, maybe it was only a trick of the firelight, she looked softer and even vulnerable, in a feminine way. And there was no mistaking a tiny smile that upcurled the corners of her lips. "But I believe you'd best let it go at that . . ."

Not listening now, he reached out, pulled her against him, and kissed her. In the back of his mind, he felt a flicker of surprise at her response. It wasn't overwhelming, but it lasted a few heartbeats before she pushed him firmly away.

"Why did you do that?"

Lazlo felt the hotness in his face. "I thought maybe you needed it. Or you would like it. Maybe I just wanted to. I don't know. Good night."

He turned and tramped away, but her voice brought him to a halt. "Mr. Kusik—"

"Yes."

"I did like it," she said very gently. "But don't do it again. Good night."

* * *

The next day's journey was far tougher than any that had gone before.

It got worse as the day stretched on and all their early steam ran out of them. Even where the snow hadn't piled too heavily, it was like slogging through a shallow lake of molasses. In places where the snow had drifted deeply, they bucked through by sheer force. The mules strained at their harness while the children hoorawed them.

Tying up with this party had been a wise move of his, Lazlo decided. Alone he never could have gotten past the worst stretches. Time and again he, Mark Bly, and several husky youngsters found their combined strength taxed in lifting the wagons bodily to get them across bad spots and rolling again.

Mark commented on the unusual difficulty of tussling Lazlo's apparently light wagon into line with the others: "Gadfrey, Mr. Kusik, this outfit of yours must weigh a ton! If I didn't know better, I'd swear you were toting all the crown jewels of Europe and their royal wearers too."

The observation didn't worry Lazlo. Mark was too innocent to suspect the real nature of Lazlo's cargo, and he had an inexhaustible good humor that extended to everything except the fact that pretty Cissie O'Halloran seemed constantly to linger in his vicinity. The young girl obviously had a case on Mark Bly, and he just as obviously was flustered and embarrassed by it.

By nightfall the weather was turning stone-cold. That was good in a way. No more snow was likely to fall while it stayed this cold, and the gusting winds finally thinned away and died off completely.

When they made camp in the early dusk, the mountain heights all around were clear, still, and dead-cold. It was a good while before the roaring fires they built up began to thaw the numbness of chill and exhaustion that seemed to penetrate to their bones.

Again, after the tired kids were bedded down, the three grown-ups crouched around a dying fire, drinking coffee and talking.

Earlier in the day, Lazlo and Aretha Bly had been quite constrained with each other. By now they were both so raveled with weariness that neither could dredge up any real feeling about their small interlude last night. All that any of them felt right now was drowsy gratitude at having gotten through a long day and being done with it.

Mark gave voice to the unspoken thought in a wry, oblique way. "Well, we didn't make very good time today, did we?"

"Not very good," said Lazlo. "Still we are a good three fourths of the way across."

Miss Aretha said quietly, "And how will it be up ahead? Better or worse, do you think?"

"It will not be better, that is for sure. But we are this far."

A lame sort of answer. Said not to deceive them, only to soften a harsh fact. The last remaining miles would be across very bad terrain. With drifting snow it would be worse yet but no telling how much worse.

Miss Aretha's glance at him was sober, friendly, and tired. "Oh," she said, that faint upcurling of a smile on her lips, "then things don't look *altogether* badly for us, I take it?"

"I think that is right, yes. If . . ."

Lazlo let his voice trail off into silence. He did not look up or around.

The noise had been soft but distinct in the crisp stillness. A sound of snow crunching under a footstep. Maybe one of the children leaving a wagon to relieve himself or herself in the dark. But he could have sworn the sound had come from beyond the square of drawn-up wagons.

Their camp was in a pocket of looming boulders on the gradual slope of a mountain base. The tall, snow-capped rocks provided a sort of cozy enclosure for the site but also might lend cover to anyone stealing up on the camp. Lazlo inwardly cursed his own thoughtlessness. Dead tired, he hadn't given thought to posting a shift of guards that night. Any danger Hutch might have posed now seemed far behind them.

But was it? Driven by his rage, Hutch might have followed them even this far, biding his time.

Mark cleared his throat. "You were saying . . . ?"

"Be quiet," Lazlo said mildly. "Maybe we are being watched. Don't look up. Don't say anything. Stay like you are."

Idly he turned his own gaze away from the fire. A man looking at fire was blinded for a few precious seconds if he peered suddenly at darkness. Now he heard it again, sure and unmistakable: the crunch of a heavy boot in fresh snow.

Fool! he thought fiercely. He had left his rifle in his wagon, and it was a good twenty paces away. They were unarmed and in plain sight of whoever . . .

Again the crunching sound, but now from the *other* side of the camp. *More than one?* Lazlo didn't let his thoughts dwell on the fact. He had to make his move now, and he must be easy and casual or he might never finish it.

He got to his feet and stretched, then turned and strolled toward the wagons. The flesh of his back crawled. Sweat stood icy on his face. He had the feeling, bone-deep and sure, that if he'd ever stood in mortal peril, it was here and now.

He came against the sideboard of his wagon and very casually reached under the seat, closing a hand over the stock of his Winchester.

A bullet smashed into the sideboard inches from his elbow. The whipcrack of a gunshot beat down the stillness.

Before the craggy echoes died away, Lazlo had yanked his rifle free and was melting to the ground. Rolling sideways under the wagon and into its deep shadow, he levered the rifle as a second shot chewed up snow and flung it stinging into his face.

CHAPTER 14

Lazlo saw the orange flare of gun flame from the camp's edge
and fired at it. There was a bawl of pain or anger: he was on
target or close. At the same time Lazlo rolled sideways again,
pumping the lever, firing.

A man yelled out there, this time giving a garbled order, and
now guns opened up from three sides, all the firing directed at
Lazlo's position. He rolled out on the wagon's other side,
lunged to his feet and across the squared enclosure, and
scrambled out under the opposite wagon. With the square of
wagons cutting between him and the firelight, he ran for the
rocks, bending low. He dived for the nearest one and saw, too
late, someone's dark form crouched behind it.

Lazlo veered at the last moment; he slammed into the man
full tilt and bowled him over. He couldn't make out the face
and, in the flurry of the moment, didn't try to. He swung his
rifle in a tight savage arc that ended against the man's skull
and broke off his choked cry. He went limp.

A pistol gleamed in his loose fist; Lazlo kicked it away. He
wondered only fleetingly why the fellow hadn't cut him down
before he reached the boulder.

Lazlo flattened against the rock, levering his rifle again, just
as a running figure crossed the clearing and was briefly limned
by the firelight before it reached the square of wagons and was
lost in its shadow.

Damn! He could not shoot in hopes of drawing that one's fire.
Not with all those kids bedded in the wagons. They were fully
awake now, and their shrill lift of voices was querulous and
scared.

"You kids stay in the wagons!" Lazlo roared. *"Don't come out! Stay like you are!"*

His yell drew fire from at least two hidden rifles. One bullet spanged off his sheltering boulder. All he could make out were powder flashes off in the rocks. He returned fire at both, but it was blind shooting.

It wasn't pitch-dark. The sky was clear, a dark cobalt blue in color, and the stars were bright. They laid a milky sheen on the snow cover that reflected much of the surrounding scene, now that his eyes were accustomed to the off-shade light. But the shadows deeply swallowed whatever lay within them.

Now at least he was on even terms with these people. But who were they? *Christ!* The Blys must still be crouched by the fire, helpless and exposed to gunfire, and so were the children in the wagons.

That, in a way, made Lazlo Kusik just as helpless.

The thought had hardly crossed his mind when a child's shrill cry split the abrupt silence. Then there was a man's calm voice, like silk over steel. It came from the wagon square.

"I advise you to stay as you are, my friend. Don't move. Just listen. I have taken one of these budding blossoms of the slums in hand. I have a pistol set against its head."

The sharp *snap* of a pistol hammer being cocked rose above the children's whimperings. Lazlo strained his eyes against the shadows. He could make out nothing inside the square.

"I will twist the child's arm," the voice went on in the same dead calm way. "Listen."

There was a short childish scream of anguish.

"Do you believe what I say?"

"Yes," Lazlo said hoarsely. "All right."

"What you will do, then, is step out and come this way with your hands high and no weapons in them. I will give you ten seconds to do so. If I do not detect a sign of compliance after my count of ten, I will pull the trigger."

Lazlo didn't know the voice. But he knew with an icy and absolute certainty that this was no bluff.

"Yes! All right, I am coming!"

Maybe to be shot down the moment he showed himself.

That tug of alarm gave him a moment's pause, and then he heard the man he'd slugged groan with returning consciousness.

Maybe, he thought, *they would shoot me but not risk shooting him too.* Lazlo laid down his rifle, bent and grabbed the man's wrists, and hauled him upright. The man's head lolled back; starlight fell on his face. Robert Topbear. Lazlo caught the reek of whiskey, and then he knew why Topbear had not shot at him. Topbear had been stone drunk.

Lazlo ducked his shoulders and let Robert Topbear collapse across them. He tramped slowly out from his shelter, around the wagons, and over to the fire, where the Blys still crouched, frozen in place by a violence with which they couldn't cope.

"Show yourselves!" Lazlo yelled in a burst of fury and frustration. "Damn all of you, show your skulking faces!"

"We are about to, Mr. Kusik!"

The orotund and genial voice of Colonel Laban Ruddy rolled out of the dark. "Now, if you will lower Mr. Topbear to the ground. Nobody will open fire on you. Gently, if you please . . . That's it. Hands high above your head now. Splendid."

Laban and his companions came out of their places among the boulders and into the firelight.

They must have surrounded the camp with an ignominious ease. Coming up the trail, they would have spotted the campfire and then, aided by starshine on fresh snow, spread out and eased themselves into various positions among the rocks. All seven of them.

Lazlo felt only a dull surprise at seeing Hutch Prouter among them. How else could they have managed to follow his trail?

Laban Ruddy motioned at the Blys with his rifle. "Up—up. Surely a pair of bluestockings such as I'm told you are know how to receive guests properly. Come, on your feet."

"'Guests!'" Miss Aretha stood up, small and very straight, angry color in her face. "You assault our camp like brigands and call yourselves *guests?*"

"A hundred pardons, dear lady." Laban inclined his head.

"The expected intransigence of our friend Mr. Kusik made a clandestine approach unavoidable. Search his clothing, Mr. Jacks, will you? Might have a nasty trifle or two concealed on him. Keep those hands well above your head, Mr. Kusik."

The slight, mild-faced man—the only member of the party Lazlo hadn't seen before—came over to Lazlo and began to search him. Moving like a snake, smoothly and lithely, he did it quickly and expertly. He turned up Lazlo's Bowie knife and jackknife and then stepped away.

Robert Topbear raised himself on his hands and vomited. He got unsteadily to his feet, rubbing his head and looking rheumily around him.

"Everything's in hand, Robert," Laban said coldly. "No thanks to you. Go and lie down somewhere. It's what you seem to do best . . . You—the Blys, is it?—get those children out here and over by the fire. And stop their damned caterwauling! Bije, Mr. Prouter, go with them. And search those wagons for any weapons."

Hutch stood hulking in the orange leap of light. His eyes were bleary and bloodshot; a wicked grin split his bearded lips. He was savoring this moment.

Again, silently, Lazlo raged at his own negligence. Something that hadn't crossed his mind was that Hutch might return to Bozetown and make common cause with Ruddy. For all of them to catch up with the Bly party so quickly, even allowing for how long it had taken Hutch to tramp back to Bozetown and make alliance with Laban, they must have come on horseback. Once they had spotted the camp, they would have tethered the horses back on the trail and then stolen in on foot.

Hutch lumbered along behind Miss Aretha and Mark as they headed for the wagons. Bije Willet followed them, taking his eyes off Lazlo for the first time.

Another one who would like to cut out my heart, Lazlo thought almost wearily. Hutch and Ruddy and him. It was just a case of who got his execution in first.

Laban Ruddy smiled his genial smile. "Well, Mr. Kusik, didn't I assure you we would meet again? Beg pardon . . . I've neglected to perform the amenities. Mr. Kusik, may I present

Mr. Creed Jacks, who has discovered an interest in common with me. And Mr. Prouter."

Creed Jacks. The name rang a bell at once. Those top guns who frequented the remote camps weren't so many in number that their names didn't often come up wherever men got together to swap trail gossip. Considering his reputation, Jacks looked colorless, almost ineffectual.

But he did things with a terrifying precision. He had been ready to kill a child. God, the man was worse than the others put together!

Lazlo turned his head enough to catch Sureshot Stell in the corner of his eye. She had added a heavy Mackinaw coat to her rough man's costume and beneath her hat wore a thick scarf tied under her chin to protect her ears from frostbite. She held her rifle on him with a negligent ease. The stony set of her face was uncompromising.

She must have gotten a dandy account from her daddy about how her cousin Ab had died at Lazlo's hand. And for damned sure nothing in it would have put Lazlo Kusik in a good light.

Tipping his head the other way, Lazlo studied the colonel's younger daughter, Myra Mae ("The Princess"). She looked as toughly primed as her sister. Now dressed in a man's clothing much like Stell's, with a droopy slouch hat that partly shadowed her face, Myra Mae held a rifle on him exactly as if she knew how to use it.

The children were rousted out of the wagons and herded into a group by the fire. Most of them were blinking and confused; some looked defiant. The youngest ones were softly whimpering. The oldest boys looked both downcast and sullen, no doubt ashamed of their failure to bring the handful of guns into play at the first hint of danger. But none of them were to blame. The sudden invasion of the camp might have paralyzed any grown man. All that resistance would have gotten them was being shot down.

"Shut those brats up," Laban said impatiently. "We don't intend them any harm. Get that through their heads, will you?"

Miss Aretha's gaze snapped with a blue and bitter fire. "Perhaps I might," she said icily, "if I could only believe it myself."

"Madam, I have no designs on anyone's life. With a single possible exception." Laban's glance shuttled briefly and wickedly to Lazlo. To his nephew: "Bije, fetch our horses in and tend them, will you? Now, Mr. Prouter, why don't you put your theory—and your brawn—to the test? Go tear the endboards off that wagon of Mr. Kusik's, and we'll see just what—"

Laban was interrupted by a fit of coughing from Myra Mae. She bent over and dropped to her knees, her body wracked by the violence of the attack.

"Myra?"

"It's all right, Pa. I'm all right."

Stella took a step toward her. Myra Mae motioned her sister back with an irritated gesture. Slowly she straightened and dragged herself back to her feet, her jaw set and rifle trained. But she was shuddering all over. Her face was blotchy, and her eyes were glazed from the coughing attack.

Or maybe from worse.

It took Hutch only a few seconds to rip off the nailed-on tailgate of Lazlo's wagon with his bare hands. It took him a couple of minutes—by simply grabbing and raising up the front of the wagon and using his enormous strength—to shake the contents of the false bottom out on the ground.

Lazlo's strike. There was the proof of it, glittering in the snow at their feet, polished to a rich promise by the fire. It occupied the avaricious attention of Laban, Hutch, and Creed Jacks for a brief time. They picked up chunks of ore and turned them in their hands, while Laban's daughters went on holding Lazlo at gunpoint.

Laban tramped back to the fire and halted a few feet from Lazlo. A cold venom etched his warm and plummy tones. "Well, Mr. Kusik, we've gotten a part of what we came after. Can you think of a good reason why we shouldn't have the rest of it?"

"I take that to mean my life."

The lack of concern in Lazlo's reply seemed to touch a raw nerve in the colonel. "That—exactly! A life for a life. Why not?"

"Because then," Lazlo said calmly, "you will not get the rest of the gold."

"The rest . . ." Laban's brow wrinkled; his eyes narrowed. "More gold than this?"

"What you see here is what little I could take out in one load. Yes, there is more. I hid it. And your tame Indian could not find it, so I guess I hid it pretty good, eh?"

"More gold," Laban murmured. "How much more?"

Lazlo shrugged. "Four, five times as much. I cached all of it away to come back for later. Maybe there is a lot more on my claim that I did not turn up. Still, the claim is in my name. This is something to think about, eh?"

Laban stared at him a long moment. Hutch stood by, scowling, and Creed Jacks's face was expressionless. The short silence was broken only by a crackle of flames.

"I think," Creed Jacks said quietly, dryly, "we might hold our horses a bit. I should like to hear the man's proposition."

Hutch stirred ominously, grunting, "Shitmaroo. This hunky son of a bitch is looking for a way out. I wouldn't trust him no way whatever. Sure, that is what he's doing by God, stalling for time."

"Possibly," said Creed Jacks. "Quite possibly, Mr. Prouter. But as I say . . ."

Laban tugged at his goatee. "We can listen at least. Very well, Kusik. Have your say. What do you want?"

"To stay alive. To keep these people alive also."

Lazlo nodded toward the Blys and the children. Miss Aretha's chill and angry gaze met his. No doubt she was thinking, now that his hidden cargo was revealed, that he'd taken advantage of them to get his gold across the mountains. True enough, but they had benefited too. Let her think of that.

"Reasonable," said Creed Jacks. "But their lives are not at stake. Only yours."

Lazlo shook his head. "The trails up here twist every which way. Now the snow has blown them over. These people need me to lead them across. They want to go to Carson's Crossing. Why don't we all go there? Now it is a lot closer than Bozetown. And the gold can just as well be sold there."

Creed Jacks showed the wintry wisp of a smile. "True . . . true. But we don't know the trails up ahead, sir. We've trusted Mr. Prouter to guide us this far . . ."

"And I will guide you the rest of the way. I brought everyone this far, eh? I know the trails."

"So do I, you hunky bastard," growled Hutch.

Lazlo looked at him and smiled. "That is right, big pard. If they can keep you sober that far."

Creed Jacks flicked a warning glance at Hutch. "Go on," he murmured.

"I will lead you across all right," said Lazlo. "But there is rough going ahead. We will need all the strong arms we can muster, even those of the kids, to get the load of gold through. If we all go together, we'll be sure of making it, eh? And you will get all you want."

"And what," Creed Jacks said affably, "is 'all'? Clarify your terms, sir."

Somehow Jacks had slipped into complete command. It was as though Laban, Hutch, and the others had been washed into the background. Avoiding Jacks's eyes, Laban got a flask out of his pocket and took a pull at it. Hutch glowered and said nothing. Neither did Bije. Lazlo shared their feeling. Meeting Creed Jacks's opaque stare, he felt sweat dampen his clothing to his skin.

"Well, it is simple," he said. "The gold in my wagon is yours. The gold I left hid on my claim is yours. So is the claim itself. A quitclaim can be made out to sign it over to you . . . to whoever you want. Maybe all of you, eh?"

"Well enough," said Creed Jacks. "Provided you are not bluffing, I should hate to say lying, about that hidden cache of gold."

"Of course I cannot say how much gold I may *not* have found. But that which I found and left—it is there. Waiting."

Creed Jacks grinned. "And it is really 'four or five times' what's contained in your wagon?"

Lazlo forced a grin of his own. "Well, maybe I exaggerated a little. But not much. What's left is a lot more than I could pack out in one trip. And you will not know *where* it is till I show you, eh?"

"And meantime we depend on your word for all this?"

"No more than I depend on yours." Lazlo paused. He tipped his head toward Hutch and Laban and Bije. "These three want to see me dead. I will depend on you to see that they are disappointed."

Creed Jacks's wispy grin turned to a laugh. It was thin, shallow, and not very amused. "Quite agreeable to me. I trust Mr. Ruddy and Mr. Prouter will also find it so."

A long pause, during which Jacks didn't trouble to glance at his partners. Neither of them commented.

"That being the case," Jacks went on, "we'll proceed as you suggest. One thing, however. You are a fighter, Mr. Kusik. It shows in every move you make. In every lineament of your face. It is not in your grain to yield the whole pot—particularly as rich a one as you've tantalized us with—so glibly and easily."

Jacks smiled through an even longer pause. It lasted maybe ten seconds. Lazlo merely stared back at him. There was nothing to say.

"The reason, of course," said Jacks, "is patently obvious. You have now gained yourself a little extra time. You'll wait on happenstance to provide a fillip of diversion that might enable you to turn tables on us. On *me*. When it occurs, you think you will seize your advantage. When you do, Mr. Kusik . . ."

Jacks pushed back the skirt of his sheepskin coat and tapped a forefinger on the butt of his pistol. "When you do, you will be dead. Do you understand me? Instantly dead."

CHAPTER 15

As Creed Jacks had readily guessed, Lazlo had given up so easily because he'd every intention of watching for his chance to catch Jacks and his party off guard. Now he privately, wryly, admitted to himself how slight that chance was. But he'd try if he could. Jacks was right. He was made that way. Even if all odds were against him, he was damned if he'd yield all that he'd slaved and sweated out his guts to realize: the strike of a lifetime.

Not even if resistance cost him his life.

Probably it would. Jacks's party had complete control of the situation. All the weapons were in their possession. They had solidarity—of a sort. Laban and Hutch might resent Jacks's assumption of leadership, but they'd accept it, and whatever Laban accepted, Bije, Robert Topbear, and the daughters would also accept.

Lazlo hadn't the least confidence, anyway, that Jacks would keep him alive a moment longer than necessary to cinch the location of the gold ore back on his claim. *Why should he?* Lazlo thought coldly. *I would not in his place.* Maybe he was not the same kind of man as Jacks, but he understood that kind of man only too well.

The wagons were rolling out as the bleak dawn broke, making their slow way up the tortured windings of old mountain trails overlaid with only a little snow in some places, deeply drifted in others. A cutting wind built up through the long gray day, skirling the snow in biting gusts that slashed at their faces and then settled, only to kick up again.

The higher they advanced into this last treacherous arm of the western Elks, the more difficult the going became. With three quarters of the distance to Carson's Crossing already covered, they were now held to a snail's crawl next to the ground they had covered on previous days.

More and more often the line of wagons was stalled by the necessity to boost them, one by one, over rock- and snow-laden parts of the trail. Hutch and Bije added a lot of welcome muscle to the effort, and every bit of it was needed.

It wasn't a congenial day in any sense. The biting cold and bitterly rough trail would have ensured as much. Meantime, the entire company was divided against itself. The only goal they held in common was getting across the peaks. And Lazlo had the sure and cruel knowledge that no one person of the party was regarded with more suspicion or downright hatred than he was.

Only Mark Bly didn't seem to share the general animus toward him. For most of the day Lazlo and Mark plodded along side by side, their faces bent against the blizzardy blasts. Sometimes they talked, often raising their voices against the cutting swell of wind.

"Sorry everything had to turn out as it did, Mr. Kusik," Mark ventured.

"No sorrier than I am," Lazlo said grimly. "It is the breaks of the game."

"My sister, I'm afraid, hasn't altogether thought through your side of the matter. She appears to feel that, well, you have used us in a way."

"She is right. No blame to her for that."

"But it's not that simple!"

"Nothing ever is."

Mark gave Lazlo a brief and baffled glance. For a half-minute, he bent his head out of the wind and then said hesitantly, "Mr. Kusik . . . is it true what you told these fellows about the gold that is still on your claim?"

"Yes," Lazlo said wearily, "it is true."

"Then it'll be all right with you, won't it? I mean—of course it's outrageous that you should lose all the fruits of your labor. But at least you'll stay alive."

"Yes, that is a very good thing."

The irony was lost on Mark. His thoughts were already veering on another tack. It took him a few more minutes to come out with it, sort of obliquely: "That girl . . . Myra Mae. She's very sick, isn't she?"

"I would say so. When they cough like she does, like they are throwing up their insides, usually they are very bad. We call them 'lungers.' The best thing for them is to winter in a dry place with a good warm climate."

"Yes, so I've heard." Mark was silent for another interval as they tramped along. Then he burst out: "What a damned shame! A lovely girl like that . . . and her life wasting away. Mostly on account of her father's greed!"

Lazlo gave him a brief, mild and wondering look. "Sure. It is too bad, all right . . ."

By early afternoon the wagons crossed the highest point of their journey, a saddle-shaped dip between two peaks, and started down its other side. Ahead, Lazlo was pretty sure, lay the worst part of the whole trip.

So far, they had labored along an upward ascent all the way, and now they were over its hump. But it wouldn't make the going any easier. To the contrary. The steep twisting trails ahead skirted tall cliffs and followed hairpin bends that hung over sheer drop-offs. Lazlo figured that all the trails he'd mentally mapped were wide enough, even at their narrowest, to accommodate the wagons. They might run into tight squeezes here and there, but they could make it through all right.

Trouble was that the shallow fall of snow had added to the problem. In many places the footing was dangerously slick. Where wheels could otherwise take a grip on rough rock, they'd be likely to skid and slide precariously from one side to the other.

Unexpectedly, it was Laban Ruddy who supplied the know-how they needed at this point. Laban had taken the wagons of his medicine circus over all kinds of terrain and through the worst kinds of weather. Cold sober now, he offered crisp pieces of advice that made sense. He stressed the importance of not letting any of the wagons or their teams get out of control.

Once they did and were on a runaway course going downslope, nothing could stop them.

What they had to do at the bad places was to evacuate all the youngsters, even the sick ones, from the wagons. They would cut down some of the stunted mountain saplings, trim them to poles of the right length, and lash them between the wheel spokes as rough brakes. Yes, the locked wheels were sure to skid on the slippery places, but if they weren't turning, they could be controlled. There'd have to be someone on the drivers' seats to handle the reins. And a couple of men up ahead to grab the headstalls of the lead mules and steady them. It wouldn't hurt, either, to have another pair of men positioned at the back of a wagon to throw their weight on the rear wheels in case they threatened to slough out of control.

No need to hurry any of it, Laban said. The wagons could be maneuvered across the rough places one at a time. It would take them a day or so longer than expected to complete the whole journey. But they'd be sure of making it.

For the next several hours, they worked at it as Laban had suggested.

An hour or so of guiding a team and bulky wagon along the hairpin turns of trails that often verged on sheer drop-offs was enough to melt the starch out of anyone's nerves and muscles. So each of the men and older boys put in an hour-long shift apiece on a wagon seat. Sureshot Stell served her stint along with them. Lazlo drove his own heavily laden outfit, taking turns with Laban and Robert Topbear, who were the best teamsters. They wanted to take no chances with its cargo.

Robert Topbear was in a black mood all day. When he'd come groggily awake in the morning, he'd found his long braids missing. Someone had sneaked up on him in the night and cut them off. Also, Laban had clamped down on his drinking after giving him hell for being drunk when they'd taken the camp. No more of it, Laban had warned.

As sunset drew on, they were easing down away from the most precipitous stretches, and everyone was starting to relax a little—even Robert Topbear. At a stop, as Lazlo swung off his wagon to be relieved by Topbear, the Indian was almost jaunty.

"Enjoying the trip, paleface? I hope so. It's likely to be your last."

Robert Topbear tilted his head toward Creed Jacks, who was standing a ways off but always keeping a vigil on Lazlo. "Or do you believe that once that fellow has what he wants, he'll let you go free to pose a future threat to him?"

"We will see."

"That we shall!" Robert Topbear said jauntily. He climbed laboriously to the driver's seat and took up the reins, saying across his shoulder, "I'll think of you when I'm sitting in an exotic bistro in N'Awleans, dining on *omelette aux fines herbes* and *fraises de bois,* and washing them down with twenty-dollar-a-bottle champagne—name your preference. I'll even tip a glass to your memory . . ."

Lazlo narrowly wondered if Topbear had been tipping a bottle or flask during the last hour. His spirits had picked up pretty fast. It would do to keep an eye on him.

When they started rolling again, Sureshot Stell had taken over the wagon ahead of Lazlo's while Mark Bly and the husky youth named Tim brought up the last two in line. The men tramped alongside the wagons, ready for any emergency, and Lazlo stayed close to his own . . . and to Robert Topbear.

There was a bad place ahead where the trail clung to a precarious shelf that was hedged on their right by a vaulting wall of granite and, on their left, shouldered out over a nearly perpendicular drop. The trail slanted downward at a slight pitch but not enough to warrant braking the wheels. All the drivers had to do was hug the granite wall and watch themselves on the turns.

Knowing of a particularly bad one just ahead of them, Lazlo tramped up by the lead wagon and offered Sureshot Stell a word of caution. She only gave him a tight-lipped nod. He could see that she had her team under expert control.

He halted and turned back to pass the word to Robert Topbear. He surprised Topbear in the act of dropping a pint bottle into his pocket. Either he'd taken a pull at it or was about to. Lazlo started angrily toward him, but Topbear gave a defiant shake to his reins, hoorawing his team sharply ahead.

A ripple of panic ran through the mules.

Lazlo yelled, "Don't, you fool!"

Then he leaped aside, flattening himself against the granite wall as the gold wagon jolted ponderously past him.

Just forward of them, Sureshot Stell was carefully reining the mules on the sharp bend. As she began to swing around it, slowing to a crawl, Prunes and Matilda—Lazlo's mules—shied at the prospect of a sudden collision. But the weighted wagon behind them pushed them hard, and the squealing mules smashed at an angle against the rear right side of Stell's wagon.

It skewed wildly around on the slick rock and then tipped slowly outward, hung for a moment on two wheels, and crashed on its side. It didn't go over the brink of the precipice but lay tilted a foot or so from it while the mules thrashed against the tangle of their harness.

The impact brought Prunes and Matilda to a trembling, uncertain stop, with Robert Topbear sawing wildly on the reins and yelling, "Whoa!"

Lazlo was already running toward Stell's overturned wagon. It had stayed on the trail. But where was she? Thrown clear of the seat, she must have gone over the edge . . .

At first, scrambling onto the lip of the ledgerock, Lazlo saw nothing of her. And then, looking downward, he realized that she'd escaped death. But narrowly, and only for the moment.

She had tumbled maybe thirty feet down the slight outslant of the escarpment before she'd been brought up hard by a narrow ledge of rock. It had stopped her fall. But her body was twisted awkwardly across it. Any movement, even a slight one, might roll her off in a nearly straight fall down the remaining hundred or so feet to the base of the cliff.

"Don't move!" Lazlo yelled at her. "Just do not move!"

She managed to turn her face up toward him. It was set and white with pain. "Move . . . hell." She managed a husky whisper that barely reached him. "I think my arm is busted . . . Buster."

That tough streak of her humor . . . showing at a time like this! Lazlo thought, *God what a woman!* And forced a tight grin to his lips.

"Stay still," he told her. "We will get you up."

By now the others were pushing up alongside him.

The flush of cold died in Laban Ruddy's face as he looked down and saw his daughter's predicament. His face became as white as paper. "Oh, sweet Jesus. Stell . . . !"

Lazlo caught hold of his shoulder and gave him a hard shake. "Don't go faint now. Later if you need to. Now we must get her up. Do you have a rope with your stuff?"

Laban rubbed a hand across his temple. "A rope . . . a rope? Yes." He turned on his nephew. "Bije, dammit, get that cowman's rope out of our gear!" He swung back to Lazlo. "But *what?*"

"Her arm is broke, she thinks. So if we let a rope down, she cannot tie it around her. One of us must go down to her and bring her up."

Creed Jacks stood by, his flat gray eyes as bland as slate. "That should be interesting to see," he murmured. "Care to volunteer for the job, hunky?"

"I already have," said Lazlo. "All of you help me set this wagon back on its wheels."

The men pitched in to heave Stell's wagon upright, back off the rim; then they calmed the mules and cajoled them into hauling the wagon forward a few yards. It cleared off the rimrock above where Stell was stranded.

Bije came loping back with a coiled rope. Lazlo took it and shook it out: a cowman's fifty-foot lariat, never before used from the look of it. It would do fine.

Lazlo made an end of the rope fast around his torso under his arms as he gave instructions. Hutch and Bije, the two strongest of them, would hold their weights against the rope at the edge of the drop. The others would lend a pull behind them—as many of them, men and boys, as the rope's length would permit.

Hutch rolled his bloodshot eyes, grinning. "Hey there, little pard. You reckon you can trust me all that far?"

Lazlo smiled. "I think I can."

Glancing at Laban Ruddy, he said, "Colonel, can I trust you to put a bullet through my big pard's head if he lets go the rope?"

"You can," Laban declared flatly. "You can depend on it. Damn it, Kusik, get going now!"

Lazlo let himself down over the rim, gripping the rope in both hands and walking backward, feeling the strain of his weight on the tough hemp. He didn't look downward any more often than he had to. Just a glance at the almost sheer drop was enough to chill a man's guts.

Fleetingly, though, he had to look down now and again so he could maneuver himself close to Stell's side.

"All right!" he yelled at the men above. "Hold steady now!"

There wasn't enough room on the ledge for him to place his feet and settle his own weight. He would have to get Stell off it while he dangled on a rope above a free fall . . . and trust that the men's braced strength could handle their combined weight.

Sprawled on the rocky projection, Stell turned her pain-glazed eyes just enough to meet his. She whispered, "What now, Buster? Best make it good and fast because this arm is paining me something fierce. I might just go and pass out on you."

"You do," Lazlo said quietly, "and it could get a lot worse. You have one good arm, and I think we will need it to get us both out of this."

"Good. How do we do it?"

It depended on his getting both arms tightly around her waist and, if she could manage it, getting her good arm around his neck at the same time. Then they could be pulled up. All the way they would have to hold to each other as tightly as they could.

"I cannot walk back up like I did coming down," he said. "So it will be very rough."

"It was easy enough coming down for me too, Buster . . ." A grin twitched the corners of her mouth. "It's just that it hurt like hell after I got here. All right. Let's get us on up."

Somehow they managed it.

Lazlo worked himself into a position to circle her body with his thick arms while she got her sound arm fast around his neck. He had a hard time getting his right arm under her waist where it rested against the rock—and every movement cost Stell excruciating pain. Once he heard (or thought he heard) the sickening grate of bone on bone in her shattered arm. He feared she'd pass out before he could get a secure hold on her.

But she didn't. Awkwardly the two of them worked her weight over to the lip of the ledge till she rolled off it and swung heavily against him, and they clung together over the yawning gulf.

Now, with her good arm crooked as tightly as death around his neck, she managed to whisper, "All right, Buster. Best we lose no time."

"Haul away," Lazlo yelled at the men above. "And do it slow, you hear?"

It was no easy task. She was a good-sized woman, on the thin and wiry side but big-boned, and his arms grew numb as he and Stell bumped slowly upward along the flinty irregular wall. All the way Stell's face was close to his, almost bloodless with pain, her eyes and lips shut tight. But she never relaxed her grip.

Then their bodies were jogging along the rimrock and hands were dragging them up and over it.

Stell gave way to her pain and passed out almost at once. The attention of Laban, Myra Mae, and Bije was entirely on Stell. They were worried about her arm, but nobody had a clear idea of what to do about it. Then Miss Aretha pushed herself abruptly to Stell's side and knelt by her, eyes snapping.

"Get away, all of you! You'll do her more harm than anything, poking around at her. I have nursed people through sickness, and I know about broken bones . . ."

Nobody seemed to care what shape Lazlo was in, so he lay quietly on his back for a few moments. As he started to get up, Mark Bly came over and extended a hand to him. Robert Topbear, on his other side, did the same.

Lazlo grabbed their hands and they swung him to his feet.

"You're quite a fellow, Mr. Kusik," Mark said fervently. "I

swear to you—nothing in God's world could make me try such a thing as you just did!"

"You would try it," Lazlo said quietly, "if it was something had to be done. And someone had to do it. Then you would."

His gaze swiveled to Creed Jacks, standing a little ways off, his mouth fixed in a small nerveless smile. He shook his head once, as if unable to fathom all this commotion and yet mildly intrigued by it. His glance crossed Lazlo's, and his lips parted in a silent laugh.

You cold-blooded bastard, thought Lazlo. *Anybody could be alive or dead; it's all the same to you if you get what you want.*

He looked at Robert Topbear.

The Indian's brown face seemed grayish in the fading light. He met Lazlo's look stonily. Nobody but him, Lazlo was sure, had noticed Topbear's secret tippling or how it had led to an accident that had nearly cost Stell Ruddy's life.

I will say nothing, Lazlo thought. *Now it is up to him.*

The others were moving away with Stell, carrying her to a nearby wagon where Miss Aretha could properly treat her arm. Robert Topbear remained as he was, standing close to the rimrock like a man frozen in place. Lazlo lingered near him, wondering if Topbear might try something foolish.

Foolish or not, Robert Topbear did it. He fumbled in the pocket of his Mackinaw, pulled out the half-empty bottle and gazed at it a moment. A long shudder ran through him. He pulled his arm back and flung the bottle out over the gulf. It spun end over end, arced inward to meet an angle of black snow-veined rock far below, and shattered to bits.

CHAPTER 16

Aretha Bly set and splinted the broken arm as expertly as any sawbones. (Somehow, Lazlo thought, you'd expect exactly that of her.) She gave Stell a dose of laudanum from her small but well-stocked trunk of medical supplies. Very brusque and businesslike about it all, Miss Aretha then turned her attention to getting supper prepared. When Laban Ruddy tried his best to express his thanks, she all but ignored him. For once Laban's eloquence failed him; he could only stammer. From the outset she'd made no effort to conceal the icy contempt she felt for Laban and his crew, and that was enough to squelch anyone.

Maybe, too, it was why Laban showed not a fleck of gratitude to Lazlo Kusik, who hadn't expected any. Lazlo didn't blame him. Badly shaken by his daughter's brush with death, Laban was also a man sadly confused . . . trying to sort out a scramble of balances in his mind. The man he'd set out to rob and kill had saved his daughter's life.

How could he square that with himself?

Laban didn't try. At least not right away. Predictably, he took refuge in his bottle. Robert Topbear, however, held to whatever resolve he'd made for himself there on the canyon rim. Keeping himself busy helped.

When they made camp for the night, in a sheltered swale a half-mile farther on, Topbear took charge of the wood detail, sending the kids out to scare up brush and then showing them how to build their fires Indian-style, small and clean and almost smokeless. He even kept his temper when Cyrus (who else?) came capering up with Topbear's confiscated braids flapping from under the edge of his ragged cap, while he gave

out loud war whoops. Some of the other kids followed him in a
wild, leaping dance around one of the fires.

Robert Topbear watched them in tight-lipped silence. Finally his moon face broke in a rueful smile. Then a burst of
laughter rolled out of him.

Lazlo sat off by himself on his blanket roll, grinning a little
at the kids' antics, drumming the fingers of one hand on his
knee. But he felt withdrawn from all of them. His own situation hadn't changed by a whit.

Or had it? The odds against him must have softened a little.
Laban and his people, outside of Bije, couldn't help but re-
weigh their intentions toward him. That Lazlo had saved Bije's
cousin wouldn't balance off his killing of Bije's brother. Probably nothing would. But maybe Laban could keep Bije in check.

Nothing at all would sway Creed Jacks.

No matter what sort of move Lazlo made, Jacks was there,
hovering on the edge of his awareness, staying at a distance but
always in sight of him.

It would be a lot easier to circumvent Hutch, if a man got
the chance. Hutch was now steadily and sullenly drunk nearly
all the time. He shambled about the camp muttering incoher-
ently to himself. His face twitched with a bloated and bleary
hatred every time he looked at Lazlo. He was, Lazlo decided, a
man losing his grip on sanity, making him the one to watch
most of all. While Creed Jacks had an impersonal interest in
keeping Lazlo alive, Hutch was now consumed solely by a
hunger for retribution that fed on itself and grew hourly.

So did his lust for nubile young Cissie O'Halloran. He made
it so obvious with his long burning stares at the girl that finally
she retreated inside one of the wagons and stayed there.

Hard to do anything about a man just staring, no matter
what you were sure was on his mind. Briefly, earlier in the day,
Lazlo and Mark Bly had talked it over. They'd agreed to
watch out for Cissie, one of them trying to stay in her vicinity
all the time. What else could they do?

Myra Mae Ruddy came walking across the camp, straight
over to Lazlo. She stopped in front of him, saying in a half-
shy, half-embarrassed way, "My sister wants to talk to you."

"Does she. What about?"

"I just know what she said to tell you." A trace of color rose in the girl's wan face. "Mr. Kusik, I . . . well, I just want to say *I* am mighty grateful to you, anyway. For what you did for Stell."

Lazlo rose to his feet, nodding. "So then, I will—"

Myra Mae bent over in a sudden fit of coughing. When it ended and she'd straightened up to meet his gaze with a defiant, bitter stare, he went on mildly, "I will go talk to her. Thank you."

He tramped across the camp to one of the wagons, where Sureshot Stell sat on a ground tarp, wrapped in thick blankets. Her back was propped against a wagon wheel.

Lazlo halted and gazed down at her. "Hello. How are you feeling?"

"Rotten."

"Maybe you should get some sleep now."

"Sleep, hell," she said irritably. "I tried to and couldn't. God, if I could get any sleep, I'd damn well be getting it."

She leaned her head back against the wheel, shutting her eyes. Her face was colorless and drawn and tired. Her broken arm was muffled in a blanket wrapped many times around the splints and bandages. The pain must be considerable, even if dulled by laudanum. Too bad that something more up to date, like morphine, was not available.

Suddenly her eyes opened, darkly snapping at him.

"Will you for God's sake hunker down so's we can converse better? Or do you like to just stand there with your face hanging out?"

Lazlo dropped down on his haunches beside her, saying gravely, "Well, it is good to see you have changed only one way."

"Yeah. That's pretty obvious." Stell grinned very faintly. "The busted arm, huh . . . Buster?"

"No. I mean this is the first time I have not seen you with a gun or reins in your hands."

For a moment she eyed him almost angrily and then let out

a soft burst of laughter. "I reckon it is. And I reckon my days as a shootist are done with, too."

"That does not follow. Maybe the arm will heal up good as new."

"Sure. And maybe Arctic owls will winter in N'Awleans some of these times. And maybe, just maybe, I am sick to death of being a trick shot in Pa's little circus." Avoiding the question in his eyes, she tipped her head forward, lowering her gaze. "Anyway . . . reckon I just wanted to say thank you to your face. You got that coming."

Lazlo said dryly, "Thank *you.*"

"Don't you sound so damn smart!" Her eyes became hard and bleak. "You killed my cousin Ab. You expect me to just up and forget that?"

"No," he said quietly, "it is not a thing anyone forgets, ever. I never had to kill a man before. You think I will forget? How did your pa tell you it happened?"

Grudgingly, Stell told him what Laban had told her of the incident at Lazlo's claim. Robert Topbear, she added, had corroborated Laban's story.

"Mostly, then, they told you how it happened," Lazlo agreed soberly. "Save for one thing. Your cousin Ab went for his gun. I had no choice but to shoot first. Did they tell you that?"

"Well, no," she said sullenly, not meeting his eyes. "No, but even so—"

"Even so," Lazlo broke in roughly, "even if I had shot him in cold blood, he would have earned what he got. So would your pa and the others. They jumped my claim. They would let me freeze to death to get out of me what they wanted."

"All right," she muttered, "you don't need to spell it out no more."

"You believe me then?"

"Yes, damn it! What more you want?"

"That much." Lazlo rocked his weight back on his heels. "Something else too. If you want to say it. How do you like what he—your pa—and Hutch and this Jacks fellow have set out to do to me?"

Stell shook her head from side to side, slowly and wearily.

"Like? What's liking got to do with it? You think I come along on this party to help kill you and take your gold? I come along to . . . oh hell."

"To what?"

"You can believe it or not," she snapped. "I couldn't care less. What I come along for was to see if there was some way I could lend you a hand. I mean, hell, there was no way I could keep all of 'em from going after you, if they was set on it. But maybe, if I come along, I could keep 'em from going too far."

"Such as killing me, eh?"

"Yeah. All of 'em was minded to. And I wasn't about to let Pa and Bije murder a man if I could stop it." Her tone was still half-angry; she turned her gaze down. "I was damn sure there was more to the story than they told. I mean, I just never had you pegged as that sort. An honest-to-God killer."

"I am not." Lazlo picked up a handful of snow and juggled it in his palm, scowling at it. "What do your pa and his friends really mean for me then? Do you know?"

"Nothing for sure. You reckon they confide in me?" She paused, frowning. "I did catch a mite of their talk off and on. What I gathered they agreed on was letting you get this party of orphans through to Carson's Crossing, to suit your wishes. Also they would sell the gold in your wagon for current value on the market, then backtrack with you to Bozetown where you was to sign over your claim to the three of 'em—Pa and Jacks and Prouter. That's about all I got. I was pretty sure, even so, that they would try to do away with you right after that."

Lazlo nodded. Why shouldn't it work out that way? The mountain arm they were crossing formed a divide between two counties. There was a sheriff in Carson's Crossing because it was a county seat. But he wouldn't care less about what happened in a place such as Bozetown, out of his jurisdiction, so isolated it didn't even have a deputy sheriff of its own county to keep order. The county board wouldn't grant funds for such a deputy's salary. Marshal Abe Friendly was paid out of the pockets of Bozetown's own locals. Even if the authorities of either county got word that something crooked was afoot, what would they do about it?

"I reckon the same as you," he said. "Now tell me this, if you can, Stell—"

"My name's Stella. Damn it, call me that if you got to call me som'at!"

"All right. Can I ask how your pa feels about me now, since I helped you out?"

"Lord, I don't know." Stella rolled her head back against the wheel rim, tiredly. "He was so hell-afire to catch up with you. Hired horses for all of us at the Bozetown livery barn and left our wagons sheltered there, which cost a pretty penny Pa couldn't afford to pay. Not since you and Prouter and that Limey fellow won so much at our expense. Prouter and Creed Jacks, they footed our bill to the livery man, which only made Pa the madder. His pride felt stung. Now . . ."

"Now what?"

"Well, I just don't know, Buster. I reckon neither does he. I'd hazard he is more kindly disposed toward you than formerly. But when he ain't sure what he thinks, he crawls back into his bottle. Which he has done, you see."

Lazlo scrubbed a palm across his jaw in a savage wash of irritation. "Yes, I see. That way, anyhow, he is never at a loss. And if he runs low on good booze, there is always his patent medicine."

To his surprise, Stella chuckled in a quiet, friendly, tired way. "Yeah, there sure is. 'Colonel' Ruddy! He's never been a colonel of a damn thing. Ain't even a courtesy colonel like they have in the South. What the hell, though, Buster—he's still my pa. You know what I mean?"

"Yes," Lazlo said gently. "But I wonder what you think of some other things. Those nephews of his, your cousins. They killed Aussie . . . the 'Limey fellow' you mentioned."

"Pa told me. I know."

"What did you feel about that?"

"Purely sick," Stella said very quietly. "So did Myra Mae. And Bob Topbear. But Ab and Bije claimed it was an accident. Don't tell me that don't make what happened to your friend any better. I know it don't. But it's done. So what's the good of raking it up now?"

She was right. In a civilized place, civilized men would pass a civilized judgment on it all. But here?

"No good." Lazlo echoed his own thought. "Still, there is Creed Jacks." He paused, holding her eyes intensely. "He would have killed that child if I had not given up."

Stella looked down, pressing her lips together. "I know it. I had no idea of how far a man like that would go. I am pretty sure Pa didn't either."

"Now Jacks has taken over the whole game."

"Don't reckon any of us looked to that either." Stella moved her blanketed arm in a slight, angry, hopeless gesture. "Now there's not a damn thing we can do about it. I vowed I would keep a sharp eye on Mr. Jacks. But what in blazes can I do with an arm out of commission? Can't even hold a long gun now, much less shoot one."

Lazlo didn't have to look around to be sure that Creed Jacks was standing not too far off and that his stare was boring into the back of Lazlo's head.

"Can your sister? She holds a gun like she can use one."

"You blamed right she can use it. I learned her myself. And she don't hone for your scalp any more'n I do, but damned if I'd let her go up against that Jacks."

Lazlo nodded soberly. "She is a very sick girl, your sister."

"Yeah. Damn Pa! Myra Mae needs to winter-warm. But we're all of a part, us Ruddys. When Pa had to go kiting after you . . . well, even Myra Mae had to lug along."

* * *

Mark Bly had been keeping as close an eye on Myra Mae Ruddy as Creed Jacks was holding on Lazlo Kusik, only more surreptitiously. After she spoke briefly to Kusik and Kusik went over to talk with her sister, Myra stepped off by herself into the pale darkness beyond the fires.

Mark moved in that direction himself, hesitantly. Then, hearing the girl's fitful, wracking bursts of coughing, he quickened his pace. He came on her standing out of the firelight, in the lee of a great boulder, a mittened hand braced against it for support. Gradually the fit subsided and she straightened up, pulling a sleeve across her tear-streaked face. Now she saw Mark standing a few yards away—tall and gauntly awkward and not knowing what to say.

"You looking for som'at?" she said stonily.

"Oh, no." Mark moved his hands aimlessly. "Nothing. It's just . . . well, that terrible cough of yours, I wondered if there was something I—we," he amended hastily, "my sister and I, might do. She knows something of medicine."

"I saw that. She did almighty well by my sister." Tipped up, Myra Mae's pale face seemed sort of ethereal in the dimness. "I meant to thank her for that. But she ain't—isn't too approachable, you know? I allow she don't—doesn't think any too highly of our crew. Not that I blame her."

"Well," he said awkwardly, "she can be quite reserved with strangers. But she could have been an outstanding physician, had she set out to be one."

"A lady doctor?"

"There are a few of them, you know."

Myra Mae opened her mouth to reply, but the words dissolved in another terrible paroxysm of coughing. She swayed forward, and Mark moved swiftly to catch her by the shoulders. She turned her head from him as the fit went on. When it ebbed at last, she did not step away from him.

Clumsily, he took a hand from one of her shoulders, gently, so that she could draw away if she wished. But she didn't. She leaned tiredly, gratefully, against his arm and side. He felt her violent shivering even through their heavy clothing.

"Reckon I am about done up," she said quietly. "Just a question of how long I have got."

Her tone was calm and fatalistic. But under it he sensed a cry of despairing protest against the wasting of a life so brief she'd barely tasted the fruits of living. And felt the protest rise, unbidden, in his own throat and push out in sharp, angry words:

"You'll have time! My God, you must have time. You can't just . . ." He paused, swallowing. "Look, Miss Ruddy. Haven't you—or any of your family—consulted physicians?"

"Oh . . . sure." Her head stirred listlessly, a pale coil of her hair brushing his cheek. "The best that Pa could engage in N'Awleans. That's Dr. Terrebone. All he could give was advice. Good enough advice, I reckon. Mostly it came down to that I should not exert myself any more'n I had to. But our outfit travels a lot, you see, and I was not about to be left behind this season. Thought I could weather it out all right. Maybe . . . maybe I am sicker than I knew."

"I should say so! I'm surprised your father permitted . . ."

"Pa? He wanted me to stay in N'Awleans with a lady cousin of his. So did Stella. I argued something fierce and they gave in. It's just, I don't know, you get used to being with your people all the time, and you don't want to shake loose of 'em, even for a spell."

"I know," Mark said wryly.

"You do?"

"Well, I've followed my sister's lead all my life. Guess I'm of an age where I should 'shake loose,' but . . . it's a hard habit to get out of."

"It sure is," she said wearily. "I reckon that . . ."

Her voice trailed away.

Laban Ruddy had come on the scene, stepping just a little around the rock, halting for a full sight of them. Drink and anger and firelight deepened the florid hue of his face.

"May I ask, sir, what you are about?"

"Nothing at all." Carefully, Mark took his arm from the girl's shoulders and moved away from her. He felt a heavy warmth beating into his own face. "Miss Ruddy was taken with a violent cough. I hoped I might help her. I meant no harm."

"Pa—" Myra Mae began.

"Be still, girl." Laban stared fixedly at Mark for some moments. At last, slowly, the tension ran out of him.

"I believe you," he said tonelessly. "You are a gentleman, Mr. Bly. And, it's clear, hardly one of the rakish kind. But I'd prefer that you not converse with my daughter, at least in this clandestine manner. Pray don't let it happen again. Back to camp with you, girl."

Quietly and wearily, Myra Mae shook her head. "Pa, it can't

matter now, can it? He was just being nice. Why can't a boy talk to me if he wants? Why can't I talk to him? There's not a whole lot else anyone who's in the condition I am can—"

"That's not true!" Laban spoke sharply, angrily, but under his words Mark sensed a chill of fear. "Good God, Myra Mae! You're going to be all right. Do you hear? Shortly we'll be in Carson's Crossing, and we can winter there. We needn't stir from the place till you're fit! I promise—!"

He broke off.

The terrible coughing came again. Myra Mae was convulsed by it. She took a single groping step and then, like a puppet with all its strings cut, bowed over and crumpled to the ground.

But it wasn't just another fit. The girl rolled onto her back, hands scrabbling at the snow. Her whole body writhed and twisted. Her eyes were wide and unseeing, the whites of them marbled by starlight. Mark heard awful rasping sounds. Even in this bad light he could see, to his horror, the whiteness of her face darkening, swelling with congestion.

Her hands came up to her throat, fumbling and clutching, as if to tear away other, invisible hands that had already fixed on it.

"Myra!" her father screamed.

Even in that frozen moment, paralyzed by his own helplessness, Mark remembered a long-gone night of his childhood. A New York settlement house to which Aretha had been summoned, he accompanying her, where they had seen an elderly man, stricken by grippe and asthma and consumption, slowly dying before their eyes in this exact way.

Myra Mae Ruddy was strangling to death.

CHAPTER 17

Mark and Laban carried her over by one of the fires. Aretha was already hurrying up, dropping to her knees by the girl as they set her down in the flickering light. The children came running up too, murmurous and wide-eyed.

"Clear away, all of you," Aretha snapped without looking at them. "Fetch more wood here if you want to be useful. Build up this fire!"

All the kids hurried to comply.

Thank God, Mark thought fervently. *Thank God 'Retha is here to take things in hand!*

Maybe it was too late, even so.

Myra Mae's hands had dropped away from her throat. Her convulsions had ebbed to a faint twitching. Her head had turned crookedly to one side, eyelids closed and the lashes veiling her cheeks. Even the congested darkness seemed to fade out of her face except where it pulsed in the veins of her temples. Only her mouth kept working like that of a grounded fish, the guttural sounds rasping out of it with an ominous rhythm that seemed to dwindle off even as he listened.

In a dim corner of his mind, Mark noted that Lazlo Kusik had come up with Stell Ruddy leaning on his arm. The terror that Mark himself felt was mirrored on Stell's face and on Laban's too.

Myra Mae was dying before their eyes. They knew it. And knew there wasn't a thing they could do.

But Aretha was steady as steel of course. She lifted the girl's wrist and took her pulse, her own lips silently counting off the seconds. Then she looked at Laban, saying flatly: "Mr. Ruddy!"

"Yes," Laban said shakily. "My God, Miss, if there is *any-thing*—!"

"There may be," Aretha said crisply. "Is it remotely possible that your daughter has been attended recently by a physician who had ample opportunity to study her condition?"

"Why . . . yes. Dr. Terrebone—"

"Terrebone of New Orleans?"

"Yes, the same. He is—"

"I know who he is," she said impatiently. "Possibly the nation's leading authority on malaises of the respiratory tract. What did he have to say regarding the health of your daughter?"

Shaking and distraught as he was, Laban got out in a garbled way enough of what Dr. Terrebone had told him to satisfy Aretha. Essentially, Myra Mae's affliction was asthmatic rather than consumptive. Just now, probably, her throat had reached such a crucial stage of getting clogged with matter that it was choking away her life. Aretha didn't bother to say as much. Typically, all her attention was for the dying girl. But Mark knew. Knew from his remembrance of that night when, as a child, he had seen a man strangling the same way. And he also remembered how Aretha had saved the man.

Aretha turned sharply toward him. Before she could speak, he said, "You need a tube, 'Retha. A narrow tube of some kind—"

"Yes! But what is there?" Her brow furrowed. "Nothing in our supplies that will serve—"

"Just a minute."

Mark was hurrying off even as he spoke, and Aretha called after him, "Be quick! She may not have even a minute."

Mark found what he was looking for at the clearing's edge where a clump of winter-killed plants—or weeds—stuck out of the snow. He didn't know what they were and it didn't matter. All that mattered was that the stems were thin and tough and hollow. He knew as much because earlier, out of idle curiosity, he'd broken one off and examined it.

Digging out his pocketknife, he unfolded the small blade and clipped off one of the straight brown stalks. Then he cut off the upper part with its cluster of withered leaves. He peered through the six-inch reed that remained. It was clearly hollow to the end.

Mark returned to the fire and handed the stalk to Aretha. She pointed at the knife in his hand and said, "Give that a turn in the fire, Mark. Quickly!"

Mark turned the small blade several times in the flames and silently handed it to her.

By now Myra Mae was no longer moving. Only a faint noise gurgled from her throat. Aretha had already opened her coat and the collar of her shirt. Now, in a crouching position, she raised Myra Mae's head to her knees and placed the point of the blade to the base of the girl's throat.

"My God, woman!" Laban Ruddy burst out. "What in the devil are you about?"

"About, I hope," Aretha said very quietly, "to save your daughter's life, Mr. Ruddy. You may find it—"

"You'll kill her!"

"I will not kill her. But she will surely die if the substance that has filled her throat is not removed. There is no other way. You may find it harrowing to watch. I suggest you avert your eyes."

Laban's face worked with a kind of wild-eyed frenzy. But he didn't move, nor did he look away, as Aretha made a small deft incision in the girl's throat. Blood streamed down each side of her neck as Aretha sank an end of the slim pipe into the wound and set her lips to the other end.

She sucked audibly. Then turned her head and spat out a mouthful of thick yellow-white fluid stained with blood. The onlookers murmured. Dimly Mark recalled what Aretha had used that other time to save the elderly man: a hollow bamboo pen.

Aretha repeated the procedure, at the same time pressing firmly on the girl's chest with a steady rocking motion, pushing down and then letting up.

She sucked out another mouthful of discolored matter and spat it aside. Then another.

Suddenly Myra Mae's lips parted. Mark heard a deep rush-

ing sigh. God. It was working. Thank God. He felt his own
throat fill with a prayer of thanksgiving. Why should the saving
of this girl's life be so important to him? He only knew that it
was.

Barely pausing, Aretha said crisply, "Cissie!"

"Yes'm?" Cissie O'Halloran said in a hushed voice.

"You know where my sewing basket is, in the wagon. Get it,
please."

Aretha did not cease drawing up and spitting out the fluid
that had stopped up Myra Mae's throat. And she kept up the
steady in-and-out pumping of her hand on the girl's chest. Now
the yellowish poison was dwindling to a few saffron streaks in
the bright flow of blood.

Aretha pulled the reed out of Myra Mae's throat and then
turned her head sideways so the wound would drain freely.
Aretha pressed her fingers over the incision to stanch the blood
flow. Meantime she continued an even, rhythmic pressure of
her other hand to stimulate the girl's respiration.

Cissie came running back with the sewing basket.

"Thread a needle," Aretha told her. "Make haste, girl. I'll
want at least a foot of doubled thread on it . . ."

Myra Mae was still only drowsily conscious as Aretha
stitched up the muscle and tissue and skin of her throat. She
did it as quickly and neatly as another woman might have
stitched up squares of fabric over the stretch of a quilting
frame.

Everyone, all of the grown-ups and children who were
gathered around, looked on with a kind of awed wonderment.
All except Mark. He was used to this sort of thing.

Aretha, always reticent on such matters, wouldn't readily re-
veal how she'd come by the precise, lifesaving skills he'd seen
her use with an assurance that would put some certified practi-
tioners of medicine to shame. She'd always been so full of surprising revelations of that sort that over the years Mark had
ceased to wonder. Aretha had a total dedication. Maybe a lot
of it was just instinct with her. All you could do was accept and
not try to understand it.

Aretha said tiredly, "There you are, Mr. Ruddy. Your

daughter is saved. For the time being. I would suggest that as
soon as we get to Carson's Crossing, you place her in the local
hospital—I understand that some Catholic sisters have es-
tablished a very good one there—and have her remain there
until she is quite recovered. I can give you no other advice."

Laban had nothing to say. Neither did anyone else. Maybe
some of it would come out later.

Gently Aretha shifted the girl's head from her lap to a
folded blanket provided by one of the children. Then she stood
up and walked over to the fire that blazed in front of the
wagon where she and Mark had their belongings stored. She
picked up a canteen of water near the fire, took a swallow of
water from it, rinsed her mouth, and spat. She did the same
again and then wiped off the mouth of the canteen. She poured
the rest of the water into a blackened coffeepot, dumped in
some Triple X, and set the pot by the fire's edge.

Mark tramped over and halted beside her. She gave a little
start, as if roused from a private revery, and smiled at him.

"Oh . . . Mark. It went quite well, didn't it?"

"I believe it did." His tone was stiff, almost angry. " 'Retha
. . . will you for God's sake say out loud what you're thinking?"

"All right." She shook her head once, gently and tiredly.
"You're fond of that girl, aren't you?"

"Yes."

"May I ask why?"

"I don't know," he said woodenly.

Nor did he. Myra Mae Ruddy was very pretty—no, she was
a truly lovely girl—and her being ill and despairing had made
him feel protective toward her. Otherwise she didn't seem ex-
ceptional in any way. A very ordinary girl and practically a
stranger to him. Also, to judge from appearances, she didn't
come from anything like worthwhile blood.

No need to say any of this to Aretha. She'd know. What he
did say, quietly and stubbornly, was: "None of it makes any
difference, 'Retha. I can't say why. That's how it is."

"Very well, Mark." She brushed a hand across the soaked

skirt of her dress. "Goodness, all this blood! I guess I had better go and change—"

" 'Retha!"

Mark said it so sharply that she turned her head and looked straight at him. He went on doggedly, " 'Retha, I think Miss Ruddy is a pure girl. Notwithstanding her . . . relatives, I believe she is."

"Oh Mark . . ." Aretha bent her head, again gently shaking it. Suddenly he realized she was quietly laughing. "Do you know something? It's only to the impure that all things are impure."

Mark stared at her in a baffled and slightly outraged way. "What do you mean?"

"Mark, dear, listen. Through all your growing up, you accompanied me I don't know how many times on my calls to settlement houses and the like. Don't you think I've seen it all? The whole range of the human condition? And haven't *you?*"

"Well . . ."

"As to the kind of thing a man and woman can find between them, I believe I understand it well enough. I can even feel it in a way. But"—her hands made a small graceful movement of negation—"it is just not in my stars. Do you understand? I can't go that way. If you can, all blessings to you!"

Mark swallowed. " 'Retha . . . what are you saying, exactly?"

"That it's about time you cut free of my apron strings. It's just that up till now, you've never given me a hint that you cared to. If you can now, Mark, do it!"

"Even if I . . . oh hell! Even if I made a big mistake?"

"Of course you might. But that's the chance one takes. No matter what course you pursue, you take that chance always." Smiling, she stood up and took hold of his arms, giving him a little shake. "You know what's worried me more than anything where you're concerned? That you might always be inclined to follow in my steps. And you can't. It's no way of life for a man. Now, don't you think you've enough to sleep on and think about? And wouldn't you care for a cup of coffee?"

"Coffee. Sure, fine." Mark gazed at her for a long, wondering moment. "You know, 'Retha, we've known each other all our lives—"

"All your life, boy, don't you mean?"

"I guess I do," he said dryly. "What gets me is that after all that time, you can still fetch me a mighty surprise."

*   *   *

The group around the fire broke up. The kids straggled back to the wagons and made their preparations for sleep. Laban and Bije carried Myra Mae to their wagon and put her inside in a nest of blankets. Stella climbed into the wagon beside her, saying that she couldn't sleep anyway so she might as well sit up and watch over her sister.

Creed Jacks told Lazlo Kusik to turn in too; he made sure that Lazlo spread his soogans close to a fire where Jacks could readily keep him in sight.

Laban had a bad case of the shakes as he hunkered down by a fire and took a drink from his flask. For once, he had a good reason for slugging it down other than the fact he just liked to drink. It was too much for a man to take in all at once, he thought miserably. Who would have believed that so many things could become turned around in a few short hours?

He owed Lazlo Kusik for Stella's life. On Myra Mae's account, there was Aretha Bly to thank. And her brother too.

None of it, Laban knew in savage self-recrimination, need have happened. If only he hadn't kited off after Kusik in a frenzy for revenge . . . and Kusik's gold. Otherwise they'd be well out of this desolate frozen country by now. Back to a better climate where, providentially, a sound treatment for Myra Mae's illness might still be found.

Laban groaned aloud and pounded a gloved fist on his knee.

"Thinking on this 'n' that, are you, partner?"

Creed Jacks spoke lightly, settling on his haunches on the other side of the fire. He rubbed his hands together and held them to the heat, palms out. His eyes were lambent in the orange light.

Laban took another pull at his flask. "You might say that, Mr. Jacks."

Creed Jacks glanced at Hutch and Bije, who were standing a little way off, sullenly eyeing the two of them. Robert Topbear was nearby, his moon face an inscrutable mask.

"Very well, Colonel. Would you care to say your piece here and now in front of all concerned?"

"If you want."

"I want."

Creed Jacks beckoned to Hutch, who shambled over and stood by the fire, his eyes bloodshot and surly. Slowly now, Bije drifted up beside Hutch and in another moment so did Robert Topbear.

"Now," Creed Jacks said pleasantly, "we're all friends here, *bueno compadres,* partners and fellow conspirators. That sort of thing, eh? Let's have it straight out, Colonel. With a title like that, you should exert a voice of authority. Pipe up right now, won't you?"

Even in his fog of liquor, Laban felt a needle of fear as he met Creed Jacks's show-nothing eyes. But a core of determination hardened in him.

"I want to call our deal off, Jacks. Things have changed. These people . . . I am grateful to them."

"I would fancy so." Creed Jacks picked up a stick and poked at the embers, his face sallow in their glow. "Kusik and his friends saved your daughters' lives. Ergo you are prepared to forgive his killing of your nephew. And to forgo your designs on his gold. I can even comprehend why such trivia weigh so heavily with you."

Creed Jacks paused, smiling gently. "Regrettably none of it matters to me. Not by the tiniest pinch of mouse dung. Why should it?"

"Jacks—!"

"Colonel," Creed Jacks's voice cut as quietly and surely as a knife, shutting Laban off, "let us take a vote, shall we?" He glanced at Robert Topbear. "How do you feel about it, Chief?"

Robert Topbear said tonelessly, "I will go as the colonel does."

"My, what a surprise." Creed Jacks shuttled a mild glance at Hutch. "Mr. Prouter?"

"All I want," Hutch rumbled, "is to carve that hunky bastard's liver out. And that is God's truth."

"Mr. Willet?"

Bije hesitated, shifting from one foot to the other. He sent Laban an owlish and uneasy look.

There were two kinds of family loyalty, Laban thought obscurely. One kind went to your next-to-nearest kin, the other to your nearest. Lazlo Kusik had killed Bije's brother. That would be all of it for Bije, Laban knew, even before Bije muttered, "Reckon I will side with you, Mr. Jacks."

"Fine. Fine!" Creed Jacks showed all his teeth in a smile that made Laban think of bared bone. "It would seem you're outvoted, Colonel. Not, understand, that it makes a whit of difference. Just wanted to be sure you get the whole picture in, shall we say, balance. We struck a bargain at the outset, my friend. And you are going to stick to it. Right to the end of the line."

CHAPTER 18

Before the wagons started out the next morning, Lazlo walked off into the brush to relieve his bladder. He'd just finished up when a mild and sardonic voice spoke from a few yards behind him, giving him a bad start.

"Ah there, hunky! Glad to see you weren't planning to take a long walk out on us. Or, perhaps, cooking up a foolish *coup* that would only get you, and possibly some of your companions, killed. Of course," Creed Jacks added with a mild chuckle, "not being a mind reader, I can't really be sure about that last, can I?"

Lazlo shook his head. "No, not even you. Now, Mr. Jacks, you want to relieve yourself too?"

"Oh, I'm relieved, hunky. You just did it for me."

Creed Jacks stepped back and clear of the wands of brush, motioning Lazlo out too. He was very careful always not to let Lazlo get within reach of him. He followed at a distance of several yards as Lazlo tramped back toward camp.

It dovetailed with the whole animal-quick alertness of the man. Even after you turned in at night, you couldn't be sure whether Creed Jacks was asleep or pretending to be. He'd lay on his side facing you, a safe distance away but not too far, hat tilted on the side of his head to keep his face in shadow. And you could be sure—or could you?—that a gun was clamped in his fist under the blanket.

Creed Jacks was only flesh and blood. He had to relax his vigilance sometime. But how could you know when? Even if he were willing to gamble his own life, Lazlo couldn't bring himself to jeopardize the lives of all these kids who had a hope of something better for the first time. Just as surely he couldn't

endanger the lives of the Blys or the Ruddys by any action of
his.

There was a penalty, he thought heavily, for getting involved
with other people. It whittled away a man's own options almost
to nothing . . .

As the wagons inched down the crooked switchbacks out of
the mountains, the going became easier in some respects,
harder in others. A lot of snow had accumulated in the lower
passes. Not only had it pelted down more fiercely on this side
of the peaks, filling the trails deeply in some places, it had also
banked thickly along the rims and walls of the narrow canyons
through which the trails wound. The early daylight was gray,
unrelieved by even a hint of sun. It had an eerie, dispiriting
effect. Closed in by canyon walls, fighting their slow way
through drifts, both the children and grown-ups felt a depression that weighed on their minds and muscles.

Then they were on the last rough rising contour of country
that remained before the trail dipped off into the level basin
where Carson's Crossing lay. From here on they should have
easier going.

Alone of the party, Robert Topbear appeared to be on top
of the world. He was clear-eyed and sober, and getting more so
by the hour. He was still in flabby condition; it would take
months of drying out to flush the dregs of heavy boozing out of
his system if he kept to his resolve. Right now it gave Lazlo a
good feeling to watch him slogging doggedly through the drifts
and, wherever the wagons bogged down, lending all the
strength he could to helping them inch ahead.

Close to midday, a misty orb of sun showed above the
rimrock on their left side. The gray sky turned to a lighter
gray. Not a very auspicious token, but enough to pick everyone's spirits up a little. And the wagons were on a stretch that
promised easier travel.

Sureshot Stell had been riding in a wagon. Now she clambered down and tramped ahead, falling in beside Lazlo. He
was surprised at how perky she looked, even with the broken
arm, splinted and muffled and hugged awkwardly close to her

middle. Her skin was brightly flushed, but apparently from the cold and not from fever.

Politely, Lazlo wondered aloud if her arm wasn't giving her some pain.

Stella laughed. He hadn't heard her laugh before. It was a rich and satisfying sound. Sure the arm was hurting a little, but Miss Bly had splinted it up real dandy. Long as she took it easy—and who could walk very fast in all this snow?—it should be all right.

"I feel fine as froghair, otherwise. Anyways, I couldn't abide another damn minute rocking along in that wagon with a busted arm. Every time them wheels hit a jolt, a body catches it clear to her toes. How you doing, Buster?"

"I am doing all right."

Afterward, sort of tentatively, they began to draw each other out, talking about this and that. Was all of it just aimless talk? He wasn't sure at first.

One thing Stella wanted to make damn sure he understood was that after what her pa had told her a little earlier, the battle lines were clearly drawn. She and her pa and Myra Mae and Robert Topbear were all on his side.

"I had thought as much," said Lazlo. "I thank you all. But how far will this go? You might have to fight Jacks and Hutch and your cousin."

Stella laughed shortly. "Jacks fixed that. Soon's he was sure how the wind was blowing, he got hold of all the guns we had and shed 'em back on the trail somewhere. All 'cept the ones him and Bije and Hutch are toting."

"Then we are in the same boat. But they won't hurt you or yours unless any of you takes up for me. So don't do it, Stell."

"Stella, damn it!"

"Stella. I am sorry. It's a good name."

"Sure it is. Yours now, Lazlo, that sounds sort o' funny. How you spell it?"

Lazlo smiled. "In English, it is supposed to be L-a-s-z-l-o. But nobody ever got it right. When I came to this country as a kid, the immigration people spelled it wrong on my papers, and everyone has spelled it wrong since. So I myself go along with it and drop the 's.' "

"L-a-z-l-o, huh? Don't have a bad ring to it, at that."

Stella talked a little about her early life, how her pa had hoped for a son and had never made a secret of his bitter disappointment at not having one, and how out of her own hurt she'd taken to acting like a boy just to mock and anger him.

"Worked real fine," she added pensively, "so good I never sprung loose of the habit. Never really wanted to, I reckon."

"I would think your mother would put a stop to this. Didn't she ever take you in hand?"

"She tried to, for a spell. But Ma died right after Myra Mae was born. Then I took my head like I wanted and bedamned to what Pa liked or didn't."

Lazlo nodded. "It all starts there," he said thoughtfully, "when we are kids. Everything we are comes from back then."

"Ain't it the truth." She eyed him askance. "How about you, Buster?"

Lazlo told her a few things. About the early death of his father. Growing up with a mother whose grand self-puffery was her alleged descent from a great nobleman. Filling her only child with dreams of his own, a kind of silent shout flung in the teeth of the grinding poverty he'd always known.

He was sparing of details, but Stella got the idea right away.

"So finding all that gold meant a mighty heap to you, didn't it?"

"The long and short of it, Stella, is that I am a greedy man. But that, I guess, is why. Yes."

"Well, there's no pure people on either side of any fence. Leastways none I ever knew of." She laughed briefly, gazing off toward a mountaintop. "I sure ain't, myself."

"What does that mean?"

"What do you mean, what does that mean?" Her glance switched back to him, so quickly and fiercely that he knew he'd unwittingly hit a nerve. "Just what the hell you think purity *is*, Buster?"

"Well, I, uh . . ." God, how did a man get into this sort of an impasse? And once in it, how did he get himself out? "I mean," he said doggedly, "a woman is pure or she is not pure. That is all."

"It ain't by a blamed sight!" Stella balled her good hand into a fist and hit him on the shoulder hard. She was genuinely angry. "You don't know diddly-squat about anything, do you, Buster?"

Lazlo rubbed his shoulder. "Not about women," he agreed sourly. "Them I must learn more of."

"You ain't learned half by yet, that's damn sure!"

They tramped along in flinty silence for a full minute.

Then Stella, looking straight ahead of her, said tonelessly, "There was a man I met back when I was going on nineteen. He sweet-talked me a good deal and turned my head a lot. We was supposed to be wed. Then he called it off."

Lazlo shook his head, honestly mystified. "Why would he do that?"

"Why d'you *think,* damn it! Because he'd got what he wanted!"

Lazlo said, "Oh," and wisely said no more.

After another minute of tramping silently alongside him, Stella said tensely, "Anyway, I've had no use for men since then. But let me tell you, Buster. If I ever *did,* and if any man done that to me again, I would hunt him down and gutshoot him. By the Lord Harry, I would." She snapped her fingers. "Just like that!"

"It would be just," Lazlo said respectfully.

"Damn right it would. And what the hell are you *grinning* about, anyway?"

Lazlo straightened out his face. "I did not mean to grin. I was just thinking."

"Devil you was. What about?"

"About a breed of independent woman there is coming to be. Not many yet. But a few. Miss Aretha Bly is one kind; you are another. Very different kinds, I think. You are—" He paused lamely. "You are not the same at all."

Lazlo braced himself, thinking she would likely get mad all over again.

Stella only shook her head, gently puckering her lips. "No, don't reckon so. I'm noways like that lady. She is the sort will give her whole self to som'at she believes in. Am I right or not?"

"I think it is so."

"Well, that ain't me." Her gaze was set ahead, straight and hard. "There is room in my life for a man. A good man, if I ever knew one. And for having kids and raising 'em. But I tell you this." A long pause. "I won't never stand for any man telling me how I can think or say or act. Bedamned if I will!"

"I think there is room for both those things in the life of a good woman," Lazlo said gravely. "To have a family and to have her own mind too."

"You do?"

"Yes, I think so."

For quite a while they swung along the trail with no more talk. But they stayed side by side, and to both of them it felt right.

* * *

Around noon the wagons turned a jutting angle on the trail. A little farther on, they paused on the final upland lift before the long descent off the heights.

By now, just about everyone's mood was high from the increasing warmth of the sun. At the same time, busy watching their footing where melting snow and ice had turned the rock dangerously slick, they emerged onto the panoramic view almost before they knew it.

And there they came to a halt. They did it unthinkingly, involuntarily. It was a gala moment.

They were on a stretch of trail that followed a broad sweep of ledge. On one side, to their right, rose the broken spine of a granite cliff that was laced with irregular shelves of rock, rotted and crumbling. Over all of it, gleaming crests of snow had been stiffened by wind and cold into weird outthrusts of their own. On the other side, the ledge fell away in a long sheer drop of more crumbling rock faces for a hundred feet or more.

Lazlo, in spite of his own situation, couldn't blame the

younger folk for their jubilant surge of spirit. From here, at last, they could see into the verdant basin of their destination. At this height everything stood out with an incredible clarity. One could make out, distantly, like a tumble of children's blocks, the flat dark shapes of buildings in Carson's Crossing and of outlying farms and ranches.

The kids were wildly excited. Some of them showed it with childish exuberance, laughing, running, and slipping on the slick rock. Others just gaped and gazed. A few solemnly stood and looked and rubbed tears out of their eyes.

Excited or not, everyone needed the usual nooning. They needed to rest and eat. Usually they nooned with cold food. Today, Miss Aretha decreed, they would have a hot meal, for it was a celebration of sorts. She dispatched the kids in each direction, both up and down the trail, to hunt fuel for the fires. Even scrub brush grew scantily in this high, stony desolation, and it took them awhile to scratch up enough.

But that didn't matter. Haste was no longer important. The weather was bright, the season's first fall of snow melting away fast, and travel on the downslopes ahead would be easy. By this time tomorrow, they would be in the soft roll of hills that edged the basin.

The kids straggled back from their brush-rustling in twos and threes, and the fires were lighted.

Lazlo and Stella had stayed together, not making a great thing of it but keeping sort of close, talking a little as they poked around picking up a few sticks. They almost forgot everything else. In fact the two of them were downright startled when Miss Aretha came up to them, saying crisply, "Mr. Kusik, have you noticed my brother about?"

"No, ma'am, I have not."

"Well, he hasn't come back. He and young Cissie were gathering wood, I don't know which way, and nobody has seen them. I wondered if you had. Or you, Miss Ruddy?"

Lazlo's first embarrassed thought was that Mark and the girl were off spooning somewhere, but Stella's reply squelched it.

"No," Stella said slowly. "I seen one thing, though. That big pard o' yours, Lazlo. He went lumbering off up the trail a spell back. I didn't take much notice at the time, but . . . I don't think he's come back."

Both Lazlo and Miss Aretha looked at her blankly.

Stella shrugged. "Maybe it don't mean som'at. But that Hutch fellow is bad medicine. I reckon you both know it. Drunk all the time. Acting like he is gone out of his head. Was eyeing that young 'un, Cissie, pretty fierce and ugly a lot of the time."

"Oh God, he was," Miss Aretha whispered. "Mr. Kusik . . . !"

Lazlo said, "*Up* the trail it was, Stella?"

"Yes."

"Stay here, both of you. Say nothing."

As he spoke, Lazlo was already moving away from them, quickly and quietly. If nothing was amiss, no sense alarming the whole camp. If something was wrong, he must lose no time.

Damn! He should have kept an eye on Hutch as he'd resolved. His growing awareness of Stella Ruddy had caused his attention to stray.

One good thing, though: It had also caused Creed Jacks to relax his watch on Lazlo. At just the moment Lazlo was wondering where the gunman was, he saw Jacks ahead of him. He was sitting on his heels on the sunny side of a wagon, his back propped against the wheel.

Lazlo pulled to a halt. Was Jacks feigning again? He really seemed asleep, his head lolling back against the wheel felloe, mouth slightly open. This last tiring stretch of trail might have caught up with Jacks's frail constitution . . . or he might simply be bored with the sudden run of festive proceedings.

For a wild moment Lazlo thought of swiftly crossing to him and overpowering him. Just as quickly he discarded the notion. Jacks was too far away; he might snap back at any moment, and there was no time to waste. Lazlo slipped past him, giving him a wide berth, past one last wagon too, and then he raced up the trail.

Reaching the sharp bend around a bulge of rock, he heard Jacks call out warningly, "*Kusik!* Hey!"

Lazlo threw a glance over his shoulder. Jacks, somehow aroused, was starting to his feet. Lazlo shook his head and didn't slacken his run. He kept looking backward though, seeing Jacks's face distort palely, his hand slashing back the skirt of his coat.

That was as far as he got in pulling his gun. Suddenly Robert Topbear came around the wagon. He sprang at Jacks from the side and back, flinging his arms around the gunman. His rush and his weight bore Jacks to the ground.

That was all Lazlo saw. Scrambling around the bend now, he was cut off from them. Keeping up a full, driving run, he put all his attention ahead of him. His heart was pumping wildly at the end of what was maybe a hundred-yard dash along the angles of a crooked, cliff-hugging trail. Then he came to a dead stop.

He saw Mark Bly sprawled on the ground, limp and silent. A sinking dread filled Lazlo, for he was sure what else he would find.

CHAPTER 19

Mark lay in a crumpled, twisted position. At first glance he looked dead. But he wasn't. He'd been fetched a wicked blow that had mashed a great strawberry mark along the whole side of his face. Even as Lazlo bent above him, Mark moved his head and let out a faint groan. He'd be all right.

Lazlo plunged away along the trail, his boots driving fiercely at the scatter of rubble that had fallen from the rim above. Another bend was ahead. He veered around it and came on Hutch and Cissie.

The girl lay unconscious on the granite rock, most of her clothes torn away. Hutch, kneeling beside her, was tearing away the rest of them. His face was red, bloated, crazed. When he looked up, surprised at Lazlo's approach, his eyes were like raw gleaming sockets, bloodshot and out of focus.

His beard split in a great laugh. "Why howdy there, little pard! I vow, I 'uz just—"

As he said it, Hutch was swaying to his feet, pawing at the Walker Colt shoved into the waistband of his pants. Lazlo hadn't even paused. His legs pounded with a straining fury across the few yards remaining between them. Although it took him only a few seconds to reach Hutch, it seemed like an agonizing splinter of time wrenched from out of eternity.

Hutch had just dragged the Walker Colt free of his pants—he had it cocked but not yet pointed—when Lazlo's full weight slammed into him.

It was like plowing into a brick wall. Hutch's vast bulk seemed hardly to budge under the impact. In the same moment Lazlo struck blindly at the upswinging gun, caught its barrel, and gave it a desperate twist sideways as the weapon went off.

He felt the scorch of exploding powder along his cheek. The thunder of the shot, almost in his face, deafened him. The echoes clattered back and forth along the crumbling cliffside. They brought down a scatter of small debris that rained over the two men.

Clutched momentarily against Hutch's unswaying bulk, off-balance and unable to pull quickly away, Lazlo expected the sudden crush of Hutch's great hands on him. Even as the taste of despair crowded into his throat, he realized that Hutch, incredibly, was toppling backward.

Maybe it was a residual effect of Lazlo's collision with him. Or maybe it was just the final effect of all the booze he'd consumed. Whatever—Hutch was going down. And in the same instant, Lazlo thrust away from him and scrambled sideways, out of his reach.

Hutch crashed heavily on his back. But the fall seemed to clear his head, and he had retained a hold on his Walker Colt. Even as Lazlo was coming back to his feet, Hutch was climbing to his knees, cocking the Walker, swinging it up to bear. His teeth were bared, his hair dripping over his face in limp straggles.

Lazlo was half-upright before he realized how quickly Hutch had recovered. Not hesitating, Lazlo closed a fist over a hefty piece of rock and flung it as he was still in the act of getting his feet under him.

The rough-edged chunk caught Hutch squarely in the face. He let out a yowl and dropped his gun, clapping his hands over his shattered nose. He took two wobbling steps backward.

Lazlo made a wild dive for the Walker Colt. Just as wildly he grabbed it up, closed a fist around it, and, sprawled flat on his stomach, brought it up to line on Hutch.

There was no need. Hutch had staggered back a foot or so too far. Suddenly his feet were skidding away from under him. He threw himself forward, clawing wildly at the rimrock. But it was slick with ice, and he kept slipping backward.

Lazlo's last blurred glimpse of Hutch was seeing him skate helplessly on the brink, arms flailing, his beard parting in a wild shriek. Then he went over and down.

Numb and sick, Lazlo crawled over to the liprock. From there he could see the dark imprint of Hutch's body at the base of a snowy chasm far below. He must have bounced at least twice off protrusions of rock. From there on, it was a straight fall to the bottom . . .

Lazlo climbed shakily to his feet. He looked almost blankly at the Walker Colt in his fist. Then he turned to Cissie.

Apparently she wasn't really hurt; no bruise showed on her tender flesh. She must only have fainted, and already she was coming to, making soft little moans as her head turned from one side to the other. The crumple of her clothing that Hutch had torn off lay beside her, and it would be as well to let her rearrange it herself. She would not welcome the sight of any man near her as she revived.

And there was still Creed Jacks. What had happened after Robert Topbear had jumped him? No shot had been fired . . . no gun had gone off except Hutch's.

Lazlo stared at the vintage Colt. What could he do with a pistol? He'd hardly ever fired one. But at least he was armed again.

He started back down the trail at a hard trot. He came to where Mark had fallen. The youth was on his feet now, clutching at the cliff wall for support, rubbing a hand dazedly over his face.

He stared at Lazlo. "Cissie?" he said hoarsely.

Lazlo said tersely, grimly, "I think she is well enough. Hutch is dead. He did not hurt her, but he tore off her clothes. Give her a little time to cover herself; then go to her. But then you both wait, understand? Don't either of you follow me back."

Mark gave a slow, vague nod, and Lazlo went on.

He did not know what would be ahead of him, but likely it would mean shooting. He did not want Mark or Cissie in line. Christ—what chance would he stand with this antique piece of Hutch's, assuming that he could hit anything with a pistol?

Lazlo knew one thing: He would not give up again, not while he had a gun in his fist and the strength to pull the trigger.

As he drew near the campsite, Lazlo slowed his pace on the

crooked bends of trail. He went forward slowly and warily, his body sunk in a half-crouch. His nerves were so keyed that he was set to shoot at the shadow of a movement.

Skirting a sharp angle of rock, he came on Creed Jacks quite suddenly. The gunman, too, was edging around a rock shoulder in the trail, working carefully toward him.

They saw each other at the same time. Creed Jacks's gun flashed in his fist. He fired just as Lazlo jerked back to cover. The bullet scored rock so close to his face that he felt a sting of rock dust.

The shot echoes dislodged rock chips from the crumbly cliffside above. Lazlo felt them rain down on his head and shoulders.

Nevertheless he didn't hesitate. Jacks had also pulled back to shelter just after he'd fired, and in the following instant Lazlo whipped around the rock angle and flattened himself against the slight hollow beyond it, holding his cocked pistol ready.

A moment later Jacks did the same, stepping into plain sight for a moment as he came around his sheltering corner, and Lazlo fired. Not surprisingly, he made a clean miss. And now Jacks too was hugging a small hollow and cut off from Lazlo's view.

His light laugh and faint shout reached Lazlo plainly, "How do you like it now, hunky?"

Lazlo didn't like it at all. The two of them were at a standoff. The perhaps two hundred feet of distance between them was laced with abrupt outthrusts of rock and short pockets of cover. If a man were agile enough, he could either work nearer an opponent or retreat from him, dodging around the rocky projections and into the shallow depressions.

But Creed Jacks was the pistolman. Lazlo was not. Hutch's big Walker Colt felt like an unwieldy chunk of lead in his fist.

It does not matter. Now it will be one of us or the other.

Lazlo and Jacks made the same decision in the same split instant. Both men came lunging fast away from their shelters into the hollows just beyond. Both fired and both missed.

But Lazlo had missed by a couple of feet or so. He knew it

by the *feel* of the shot. And Creed Jacks, again, had come close enough to dust him with rock splinters. Now both men were cut off from one another once more.

Jacks's mocking laugh drifted to him even through the clatter of rubble falling from the granite overhangs. Lazlo shrank into his skimpy shelter, hardly aware in his panic of his own slugging pulse and the ooze of his sweat.

God. A few more shots—or even one—might bring the whole shuddering mass of age-rotted rock down on them.

Creed Jacks made the next move, springing around his shoulder of rock and firing simultaneously. His bullet screamed off a rock close to Lazlo's head, and Lazlo followed up at once, firing at Jacks as he pivoted around his own rocky angle into a fresh position.

And then it no longer mattered.

The echoes of gunfire had started to reverberate along an ever-broadening stretch of pitted cliffside. No small trickles of rubble now. Big chunks of loose rock sloughed away from the quaking escarpment and crashed downward.

Both Lazlo and Creed Jacks ducked out and away from their meager cover to avoid the falling rock. At the same time, instinctively, they fired at one another again. The merging slam of gunshots brought a thunderous groan of reply from the whole section of eroded cliff. Now, in one continual roar, a great piece of it gave way.

The main slide of rock and dirt and snow was funneling down toward Creed Jacks. Lithe as a snake, he dodged away from its path, but then he tripped and went down. The avalanche thundered over and around him. A mist of reddish dust shrouded everything.

The roar of cascading rock dwindled away.

Lazlo stood swaying on his feet. He was bleeding from a few cuts and coughing from the gritty fog that mushroomed around him. As the dust began to settle, he stumbled forward, his gun pointed ahead of him. Suddenly he glimpsed Creed Jacks on the ground through the reddish haze and drew a quick bead on him.

The Walker Colt snapped on a dead chamber. Frantically he pulled the trigger again. Nothing.

Lazlo came to a stop now, staring dully at Creed Jacks as the dust cleared away and he realized what had happened. Jacks was pinned flat, buried from the waist down in a mass of debris. He too was coughing on rock dust, and it must have got in his eyes; he was groping blindly for his pistol.

Tramping forward, Lazlo saw Jacks's gun in the rubble, maybe a yard from his outflung arm. He bent and picked it up. A finely hand-crafted weapon, it was ruined, smashed beyond repair. A falling rock must have done it. Lazlo threw the gun aside and, not sparing Jacks another glance, climbed onward over the heap of rubble.

The fallaway of crumbling granite nearly choked the trail for another hundred feet; then it tapered off, and he was hurrying on, breaking into a run as he neared the camp.

What had happened back there?

Coming hard around the last bend above the camp, he saw all of it at once. Bije Willet was holding a rifle on everyone.

He stood with his back to Lazlo's vantage, keeping all of them covered. Laban Ruddy was at the front, with Stella and Robert Topbear close to him. Behind them, watching tensely, were Aretha Bly and the gang of orphans.

It was plain enough what had happened. It crossed Lazlo's mind as a fleeting image. Bije had rescued Creed Jacks from Topbear, and then Jacks had ordered him to hold the rest of them at bay while he went ahead to deal with Lazlo.

The scrape of Lazlo's boots pulled Bije around fast, his rifle swinging with him in a cramped arc. Lazlo came to a halt. He saw the squeeze of fear, desperation, and anger in Bije's face.

Bije had come only halfway around. He couldn't cover both Lazlo and the others at the same time. The panic of indecision showed in his stupid face.

Lazlo did not raise the Walker Colt. Holding it down at his side, he said in a steely, positive voice, "Throw it away, boy. Don't make me kill you."

The Walker was jammed, or a chamber was fouled, or the

loads were spent. It didn't matter which. The gun was useless, and his words were a bluff.

Bije hesitated and then swung the rifle toward him, bawling, "Go to hell, you hunky sonbitch!"

"Bije!"

Laban Ruddy's voice cracked like a whip. He took one long step forward, causing Bije to swing the rifle back on him. "Don't try it, Bije. If you shoot Kusik, you'll have to shoot me too."

"That goes for me too, Bije," Stella said quietly. "Don't reckon you hone to wipe out all the kin you got left, do you?"

Robert Topbear put in mildly, "Nor me either. I don't think you'll do that, Bije."

Bije stared wildly from them to Lazlo and back again. He lifted the rifle high in his trembling fists and then dashed it to the ground. A kind of sob broke in his throat. "Aw right, Uncle Labe! Aw right, damn all your eyes!"

CHAPTER 20

It was not a long nooning. All of them were glad to be away from the place and to begin their last descent toward the foothills that edged the fertile basin. By sunset, as the last burn of daylight ruddied the western rim of land, they made camp in the lowland hills.

As preparations for the evening meal got underway, Lazlo tramped over to one of the covered wagons. He looked into its dimness. Creed Jacks lay on his back on a pallet of blankets, his slight body loose and sprawled. He couldn't stir a muscle below the lowest point of his spine, and he felt no sensation at all from there on down.

"Ah, hunky." Creed Jacks's face was like a blob of gray suet in the bad light, but his voice was still cool and mocking. "Come here to crow a bit, have you?"

Lazlo shook his head. "I would not do that. I think you would have got me if the cliff had not come down on you. I am sorry for it, Jacks."

"What for? I was set to get you. You were set to get me right back."

"Not this way."

It had taken most of an hour to extricate Creed Jacks from the pile of fallaway rock that had emprisoned his legs and hips. As they'd cleared away the rubble, more of it had slid down from above. At last, working with infinite care, they had freed him. Creed Jacks was in a sorry way. Both of his legs were crushed, broken in several places, and they might heal after a fashion. But the damage to his spine that had eliminated all mobility and feeling through his lower body was something else. Probably he would never walk again.

"I-believe not." Creed Jacks gave a febrile chuckle. "In any event, my working days are over . . . come what may."

"Miss Bly says there is a good hospital in Carson's Crossing. We will be there by about noon tomorrow. Maybe—"

"Quit it, hunky." Creed Jacks's grin was twisted and weary. "I'm a gambler. Been one all my life. This time I overplayed my hand. The gambler ran out his string. Happens to the best of us. Or the worst . . ."

Walking a slow circle of the camp now, Lazlo thought heavily that he should not waste sympathy on the man. But he felt a powerful depression all the same.

Miss Aretha, kneeling by a fire as she expertly fed sticks into it, looked up at his approach.

"Well," she said with a pleasant nod, "you look as though you'd lost your best friend, Mr. Kusik. I can't see why. You have gotten your gold through. From what I've gathered, it—along with what remains in your 'cache' back in Bozetown—should make you a man of moderate wealth."

Lazlo searched her words for a hint of mockery, but there was none. Her smile was sober and friendly and a little quizzical.

"Yes," he said gravely, "there is that."

"Is it Mr. Prouter? Of course you were friends—"

"No," Lazlo said wryly, "we were never that. Even if it looked so at first."

"That fellow in the wagon, then? Jacks?"

"I guess that is it. A bitter thing for a man."

Miss Aretha stood up now, her small face very serious. "It was you or him, Mr. Kusik. What he got, he asked for. 'The wages of sin . . .' Do you know?"

"Yes. But that is death. This is worse than dying, I think. There is another saying from that book. It has to do with not judging."

" 'Judge not . . .' " She paused with a prim nod. "Quite so, Mr. Kusik. I should not need reminding."

Her serious look broke in a sudden smile, making him think once again: *This woman is not plain. Not ever!* "Speaking of sayings," she went on, "there was a man of my region, a man named Thoreau. He once wrote of a friend, 'We are of different tribes, and we are not at war.' That is how you and I are."

Lazlo nodded, returning her smile. "I think it is so."

He felt less depressed, a little less tired, as he moved off and away, through the scatter of fires coming to life against the chill of night. Around them children played and laughed shrilly. Cissie O'Halloran was not frolicking. She crouched beside a fire with her arms folded around her knees, gazing across the camp.

Cissie looked up, giving him a quick shy smile that said her thanks all over again.

Lazlo solemnly touched his hat and walked on, briefly following Cissie's glance. Mark Bly was leaning his crossed arms on the tailgate of a wagon, talking to someone inside it. That was Myra Mae Ruddy, still weak from her illness.

A lot of things did not turn out as you might wish. Later on, you might smile about it, but it was never funny at the time. Least of all when you were young. Lord, the pain of being young! Goldenly reminiscing, people forgot all of it too soon . . . too easily.

Over by another fire, Laban Ruddy and Robert Topbear and Bije Willet were sitting side by side, passing a bottle (produced from God knew where) back and forth. Spotting Lazlo, both Laban and Topbear hailed him in loudly amiable tones, inviting him over to have a drink. Bije only scowled and took a long pull of whiskey.

Lazlo smiled and shook his head and walked on.

Nearly all the resolutions that men made turned out to be worth just that much, in the 'end. Still, you never knew. Perhaps since they'd all come through a fierce time, the colonel and Topbear merely felt that a little celebrating was in order. Or they were just hopeless drunks. Each was a good man in his way. Maybe that was what mattered most.

Stella was sitting with her back against the wheel of the last wagon in line, pulled up at the outer edge of darkness that rimmed the camp. It seemed to Lazlo that she was quietly waiting. Not asking for anything, not particularly expecting it either. But waiting all the same.

As Lazlo came up to her, she raised her eyes and said, "Howdy. Bet *you* ain't been that way a whole lot either."

Lazlo gazed at her, baffled. "What way?"

"No rifle. You ain't toting one about you anywhere I can see."

He laughed heartily. (How long since he'd given out a laugh that felt genuine? He couldn't remember.) He dropped to his haunches beside her, gazing aimlessly around the camp. Looking anywhere but at her.

"Maybe," he said carefully, "there is not the need anymore. Stella, can I ask—"

A smacking blow on the back of his neck made Lazlo swear furiously, swiveling around on his heels. The dark form of one of the kids was running off, and behind it trailed the taunting laugh of Cyrus.

Now it was Stella's turn to laugh.

"Say, listen. If the folks that boy is supposed to hitch up with at Carson's Crossing don't fancy him, maybe *you* could take him on. How'd that be?"

Lazlo rubbed his neck and glared at her. "I could ask you the same. What do *you* think of it? It would have to be all right for both of us."

Stella laughed again. Then she caught his meaning; the laugh faltered and died on her lips. "Listen, Buster, do you mean . . . ?"

Apparently she couldn't bring herself to say it all. But Lazlo, meeting her gaze straight on, knew once and for all that a man could find better treasures than any gold strike could offer. And it was he who said the rest.

"I mean for always," he told her.

T. V. Olsen was born in Rhinelander, Wisconsin, where he lives to this day. "My childhood was unremarkable except for an inordinate preoccupation with Zane Grey and Edgar Rice Burroughs." He had originally planned to be a comic strip artist but the stories he came up with proved far more interesting to him, and compelling, than any desire to illustrate them. Having read such accomplished Western authors as Les Savage, Jr., Luke Short, and Elmore Leonard, he began writing his first Western novel while a junior in high school. He couldn't find a publisher for it until he rewrote it after graduating from college with a Bachelor's degree from the University of Wisconsin at Stevens Point in 1955 and sent it to an agent. It was accepted by Ace Books and was published in 1956 as *Haven of the Hunted*.

Olsen went on to become one of the most widely respected and widely read authors of Western fiction in the second half of the 20th Century. Even early works such as *High Lawless* and *Gunswift* are brilliantly plotted with involving characters and situations and a simple, powerfully evocative style. Olsen went on to write such important Western novels as *The Stalking Moon* and *Arrow in the Sun* which were made into classic Western films as well, the former starring Gregory Peck and the latter under the title *Soldier Blue* starring Candice Bergen. His novels have been translated into numerous European languages, including French, Spanish, Italian, Swedish, Serbo-Croat, and Czech.

The second edition of *Twentieth Century Western Writers* concluded that "with the right press Olsen could command the position currently enjoyed by the late Louis L'Amour as America's most popular and foremost author of traditional Western novels." Any Olsen novel is guaranteed to combine drama and memorable characters with an authentic background of historical fact and an accurate portrayal of Western terrain.